# a stroke at midnight

A Collection of Gay Erotic Stories

by Johnny Miles

ISBN: 978-0-615-25443-2

# Table of Contents

# The Coffee Cart

In the late 1970s, I worked in an office building in Manhattan. The company I worked for had someone come around each day with a coffee cart, to every floor, with coffee, rolls, donuts, cookies, pastries. It was a convenience most of us considered a luxury.

Most times the cart pushers, as some of us called them, were black women. On rare occasion a black or hispanic man filled in from time to time. It wasn't the type of job that was conducive to longevity.

And then, one day, along came Juan Carlos.

Juan Carlos was from a small town in Northern Spain and had been in this country for nearly a year as a foreign exchange student when he decided to apply for citizenship. He was a dark blond with the eyes of an innocent boy and the face of an angel. His mouth was wide and generous. And every time he smiled, my body turned into liquid silver. I often wondered what it would be like to touch him and lay naked against the warmth of his slim, smooth body.

I wanted him the moment I laid eyes on him. And after a couple of weeks, I started to feel as if maybe there was something there. I couldn't quite put my finger on it, either. It might have been his smile, which I thought seemed bigger and warmer for me than for anyone else. Or it might have been his touch, which was intensely electrifying when he gave me back change and his fingertips grazed the inside the of my palm. Or perhaps it was his gaze. It lingered far too long, I thought, for him to be just a friendly straight man. I just *knew* there had to be something there and I was determined to find out.

One Friday afternoon, Juan Carlos was running particularly late. I was starting to grow anxious without his smile. I needed to see him soon.

"C'mon! Where the fuck is he?" I muttered in my office, my mind totally off the copy I had been working on. I looked at my watch. It was three-thirty; normally, Juan Carlos came at three.

*I know*, I thought to myself. *I'll just take a walk around the office until he comes.*

I threw my pencil down on the desk and got up.

*Until he comes. Hmmm. Sure wouldn't mind seeing that!*

I smiled at the thought and my dick began to stir. I briefly wondered if I had enough time to head to the men's room and whip out a quick one when the receptionist came over the loudspeaker in a heavy, Bronx accent.

"The caw-fee cawt is heah! The caw-fee cawt is *heah*!" It was a wonder to me how she ever kept her job.

I dashed out of my office and down the hallway, to the elevators. The coffee cart was stationed there, and he of the beautiful smile stood waiting.

"Hola, Juan Carlos." I greeted him in Spanish.

"Hello, my friend! How are you today?" Juan Carlos responded in English.

"Better, now that you're here. I really need this cup of coffee!" His smiled broadened as he looked into my eyes. I lingered in his gaze just a moment, then shook my head to clear my mind. I handed him the money.

"Thank you. And good afternoon." Then Juan Carlos switched to Spanish. "*Que tengas un buen día.*" He gave me a little nod and a wink.

"Gracias, Juan Carlos. You have a good day, too!" I turned and went back to my office. If I didn't get close to Juan Carlos soon, I would wind up raping him.

Sitting behind the desk, my mind kept drifting back to Juan Carlos. I kept seeing that beautiful smile, the innocent-looking eyes, and his tongue as he licked his lips seductively. I imagined him in his bedroom, half in shadows, slowly taking off his clothes. My cock hardened at the thought of him laying back in bed amidst rumpled sheets.

I tried to stop thinking about him but it was impossible; I was far too horny. I got up and walked down the hallway, praying my erection wouldn't rip through the tight slacks I was wearing.

"Back for more?" Juan Carlos said from behind his coffee cart.

3

"Oh, no! I just, um, have to go to the bathroom." I smiled at him, a little embarrassed, as if he knew what I had been thinking.

"Me too! Can you hold the door open for me? Please?" He pushed his coffee cart against the wall so it was out of the way, then faced me with that angelic smile. I swallowed nervously, thinking I saw him glance down at my crotch, but I couldn't be sure. I held the door open for him.

"Thank you," he said as he stepped past me. "I really have to go and I don't have the key for this floor." I followed behind him, nervously, then quickly stepped into a stall. I closed the door and nearly ripped my pants as I unzipped and let them fall to the ground in a pool at my feet. I sat on the toilet, my cock already hard, the shaft pulsing in my fist. My ears thumped loudly as the blood pounded in my head.

Juan Carlos stepped up to the urinal beside the stall I was in and unzipped himself. I looked at his sneakers, wishing I were standing beside him as he hauled out his Spanish meat.

Stroking my hard prick I thrilled to the sound of his urine hitting porcelain. It was strong and forceful, gushing from his piss slit. I wondered about his loads. Was he a gusher? Was he a dribbler? Was he the kind to shoot his load so far, and with such force, that he could hit the headboard?

"Ahhh! That's good." Juan Carlos sighed, pulling me out of my musing. "You know, it's bad to hold something in for so long."

"Is this going to be a philosophy lesson on the difficulties of life?" I laughed and said jokingly.

"Actually, life is simple. If you need to piss, you piss."

"Which means?" I asked, uncertain.

"It means . . ." Juan Carlos voice dropped slightly. Or perhaps I imagined it. "If you want it, take it."

"Oh, really?" So that was how it was going to be; I had to make the first move. "Interesting theory. What if you like someone and the other person doesn't know? What do you do then?"

Juan Carlos thought a moment then cleared his throat. "Then you should just go up to that person and say that you like them and would like to get to know them better."

"What if I just want to have sex?"

Juan Carlos laughed. "Is that all you want?"

"I don't know. I think I might want more. Like to have sex many times!"

"There's nothing wrong with that. They either want to have sex, too, or they don't. What's stopping you?"

I dared myself to open the stall door and lure him inside. Instead, I watched through the crack as his pants moved up and down while shaking his cock. He stuffed himself back into his pants, zipped up, then walked over to the sinks. I could still see his feet. They were turned toward me.

"Well?" Juan Carlos said coyly. When I didn't respond, he continued. "I think maybe you should just do it! That way you have no regrets."

"Uh, Juan Carlos?"

"Yes?" He was barely audible over the sound of running water as he washed his hands.

"How would you like to go out for a drink some time?"

He was silent a moment before responding. Perhaps he realized. "That would be great, but I'm afraid I don't drink."

"Oh. Well, how about a cup of coffee, then?"

"I'm afraid I don't drink coffee, either. But why don't you come over to my house? My wife is a very good cook."

"Wife?" To say I was disappointed was an understatement. Could I have read his signals wrong? "You're too young to be married." I didn't know what else to say.

"How old do you think I am?" Juan Carlos chuckled. He turned the faucet off and I could hear him drying his hands.

"Twenty-one!" I replied. He laughed again.

"Well . . . I am, how do you say? Flattered. I'm 29."

"Bullshit!"

"It's true! I'll be thirty this week."

"Oh yeah? When?"

"Tomorrow."

"No shit? Well, happy birthday! You got any fun plans to celebrate?"

"Yeah. My friends are taking me out to dinner."

"I'm sure you and your wife will have a lovely time."

My cock was throbbing madly and my balls ached for release. I stroked my thick tool and heard Juan Carlos scratch, wondering what it was that itched him.

"Let me know about going out," Juan Carlos said.

"Since you're the married one, why don't you let *me* know?" I wanted to kick myself for not being more daring or original; but now the ball was in his court.

Juan Carlos shuffled away slowly, almost as if he didn't want to leave. The door opened, then closed. I bent down and peeked underneath the stall. Through the gap beneath the bathroom door, I could see Juan Carlos' feet. He stood in the hallway, just beyond, as if hesitating. Finally, he walked away.

"Shit!" I leaned back against the toilet. Despite the discouraging news, my boner wouldn't go down. I grab my cock and cupped my balls, pulling on them and squeezing as I envisioned Juan Carlos in bed, rolling onto his stomach, exposing smooth, round buns that begged to be violated. I imagined running my hands over the curve of his buttocks, then spreading them to eat his sweet virgin hole; fucking him with my tongue, then with my thick, juicy cock. He would moan and writhe beneath me, biting his sheets to keep from crying out.

I didn't take me long since I was already so worked up. Maybe just a dozen pumps. I gasped silently as I came, spurting a load onto my belly in thick, creamy globs. Dipping my fingers into it, I then licked them, savoring the taste. I imagined that it was Juan Carlos' fuckjuice.

Later that evening, long after most everyone else had already gone to enjoy a three day weekend, I decided to call it a day. I had intended on working overtime in order to complete a rush project but I was too keyed up to get anything done. I couldn't keep my mind off Juan Carlos. And with a heat between my legs that threatened to turn into a full erection again, I gathered my stuff, left the office, and headed for the elevators.

On the ride down from the 31st floor, the elevator slowed, then stopped. The doors opened and I actually felt my heart skip a beat. I could see Juan Carlos behind the large coffee urns, pushing the coffee cart inside; his arms, slender and well-defined, straining.

"Juan Carlos!" I exclaimed with surprise in my voice. Something caught in my throat and twitched inside my pants.

He looked up and smiled. "Hey, Johnny! Staying late tonight?"

"I . . . uh . . . had a lot of work. What are you still doing here? I thought you left at five?"

"No." He shook his head. "I work until eight." Juan Carlos got the cart into the elevator, hit the button for the basement, and squeezed in beside me. The doors closed and the elevator descended.

"It's Friday night. You going out to party?" Juan Carlos stared openly at me. The nearness of him made my blood boil.

"Uh . . . no. Not tonight."

"Why not?" His left eyebrow arched slightly. "I bet you can go out to a club or a bar and get anyone you want. Have a little fun, know what I mean?" Juan Carlos winked and nudged me in the belly with his elbow. I could feel the heat emanating from his body and my breathing suddenly became a bit labored.

"I know what you mean, Juan Carlos, but I don't feel like going out."

"A guy like you should have a hot date waiting for you when you get home."

"Yeah, right!" I chuckled.

"I'm serious!" Juan Carlos said with mock hurt.

"Want to volunteer?" I quipped without thinking. There was a moment of dead silence. I swallowed nervously, realizing how it must have sounded to him. What if I had read him wrong? What if he really was just a nice straight guy being sociable?

I gulped nervously as Juan Carlos cocked his head back a bit, appearing to look stunned, then grinned.

"So you're single, right?" Juan Carlos asked curiously. I nodded. "Do you . . . live alone?" He continued questioning me. I nodded again. "You know, I lived alone for a while. In Spain. I loved it. I didn't have anyone telling me what to do or when to come home. I could bring home anyone I wanted."

"Yeah," I replied, nodding nervously. "That *is* one of the good thing about being alone."

"No," Juan Carlos countered. "The best was that I could walk around naked and nobody was there to say anything."

I gulped.

"I, uh, I take it you don't go naked in your home?" I asked nervously.

"Sadly, no." Juan Carlos shook his head.

"Doesn't your wife . . . doesn't she . . . like to see you in the nude?" I licked my lips, imagining him naked, walking around my apartment. I would never ask him to put on clothes if he didn't want to.

Juan Carlos remained silent before replying.

"She doesn't like that. She's different that way." I wanted to find out more about his home life. I suddenly got the feeling there was a lot more to his story.

The elevator stopped at the lobby and the doors opened.

Juan Carlos stepped aside so I could get off. I shrugged. "It's okay. I'll go to the basement with you. It's easier than squeezing past this thing."

Juan Carlos eyed me curiously, a slightly lop-sided grin on his face.

"Well, okay. If you don't mind." Juan Carlos pressed the basement button again. The elevator doors closed and down we went. He looked up at and smiled sweetly. I smiled back, more nervous than a teenage virgin about to get his cock sucked.

"I've never been to the basement before." I was trying hard to breathe normally. I lost my virginity in the basement of the building where I grew up so I had a thing for dark, dank, musky corners where daylight rarely penetrated.

"There's not much down here." The doors opened onto a puke green corridor illuminated by fluorescent lights. Juan Carlos stepped outside and grabbed the bar of the coffee cart. "Give it a push."

I did as he asked, holding the doors open for him as we both stepped out into the corridor. There was a hum from the lights, a knocking and hissing from the pipes that lined the walls, but otherwise, it was silent.

Juan Carlos pushed the cart silently down the hallway and I walked quietly a few steps behind him. He tossed me a smiling glance over his right shoulder.

"It's a little scary sometimes, down here." I didn't respond. "And sometimes it gets so hot! I'm sweating already. See?" Juan Carlos ran the back of his hand over his forehead and wiped it on my bare arm.

I stared at him in surprise, an unsure smile on my face. He grinned.

"You know, a wise man once told me something about life," I managed to say through my excitement and fear.

"Oh, yeah? What did he say?" Juan Carlos teased.

"He said that I should just . . . take what I wanted . . . so I could live without regrets."

Juan Carlos stopped walking and looked at me. A wicked grin suddenly spread across his face and a glint filled his eyes. I stared into them for what seemed like an eternity. I tried to speak, but found that my mouth wasn't working.

"I wonder who said that," Juan Carlos teased.

I shrugged. "Oh, I don't remember."

The corridor continued ahead but we turned right and came to a door marked KITCHEN in block, almost military style lettering. Juan Carlos reached into his pocket and pulled out a large key ring. He selected one of the keys, inserted it into the lock and opened the door. Quietly, I waited while he pushed the coffee cart inside and followed behind him.

It was a small room with a huge, walk-in refrigerator running alongside the back wall. A large metal sink, and counter was to my right, with several coffee urns waiting for the next morning.

"You know, I'm not much of a philosopher, but I would think that if your not happy at home . . ." I started.

"I never said I was unhappy." Juan Carlos opened the refrigerator door and pushed the entire coffee cart inside. Then he turned and glared defensively at me.

"I . . . uh . . . I'm sorry. I didn't mean to imply . . ."

Juan Carlos sighed. He flipped his right hand in the air without looking at me. "Don't worry about it. I

11

guess I *am* unhappy." He turned, sat down at a small desk and picked up a clipboard. He started checking things off on a list.

"Do you . . . want to talk about it?" I offered, not knowing what else to say. I shoved my hands in my pockets for fear they might reach out and grab him.

Juan Carlos looked up at me. I stared back into those angelic eyes, trying, mentally, to tell him how I felt, how much I wanted him.

For a moment, he looked as if he was about to say something, then thought better of it. I stood there, not knowing what to do. I knew I should have left, but my feet weren't moving, my legs didn't want to work. I felt he wanted me to leave, but his body language was telling me to stay.

"I'd better go," I said finally. "I'll see you on Mon- . . . I mean Tuesday. Three-day weekend, you know." I had inched my way towards the door.

"Why don't you wait? I'm almost done. I just have to change my clothes."

I sat down on the other side of the desk. After a moment, Juan Carlos stood. I watched him, my eyes darting to an obvious bulge in his pants. I swallowed hard.

He unbuttoned the mustard colored jacket he wore when making his cart rounds. Then he peeled off the tee-shirt he wore underneath. My cock stiffened as he smiled, sweet and innocent, at me.

"I guess sometimes life doesn't turn out the way we plan, huh?"

"No, I guess not." I cleared my throat as he turned his back on me. Juan Carlos unzipped his uniform pants and I watched them fall. He stepped out of them.

I pressed down on my bulging crotch as he bent over to pick them up.

"I guess I thought being married would be different."

"Is she . . . from Spain, too? Your wife?"

"Oh, no. She's from here. An American." Juan Carlos turned suddenly and caught me rubbing my cock with the palm of my hand. He didn't react. "She, uh . . . how can I say? She was something I had to do." His right hand dropped to his jockeys and he cupped his balls.

"What do you mean?"

"My visa expired." He pulled the elastic away from his belly with one hand and reached inside the pouch with the other to rearrange himself. I could see the outline of his cock against his hip, pointing to his left. I licked my lips anxiously.

"So you married her to stay in this country?"

"Oh, no! What kind of man do you think I am?"

I shrugged. "I know what kind of man I'd like you to be."

"And what kind is that?" He stepped away from the desk and walked toward me. I suddenly didn't know what to say. All those weeks of fantasizing, the conflicting signals from today had all left me dazed and confused.

"My life in Spain was very different." I looked up at him, questioning. "I was a good boy in school. The priests loved me. I had good grades, I was good at sports. Lots of friends, you know the type."

"Yeah. A goody-goody," I said and wondered where he was going with his chatter.

13

"Goody-goody?" Juan Carlos knit his brow, unsure of what I had said. He sat at the edge of the desk, right leg swinging back and forth while his obvious erection now lay closer to my face. It was all I could do to keep from reaching out.

"Yeah, you know. A goody-goody. It's what we call it here. A person who does everything by the books, the way he should or . . ." I paused and looked up at him, realizing what he meant. "Or what is expected of him. Never gets into any trouble, everyone likes him. You know. Like that."

"Okay. So I was a goody-goody. Except for one thing. And in that, I was bad." I waited for him to continue. "Some of the boys I went to school with, they liked to slap this one boy on the ass. They all said he was a *mariposa*; a butterfly."

"Why did they call him that?"

"They said he liked boys. That he sucked dick and took it up the ass."

"Did he?"

"He never did anything before. He was innocent to sex. And he was not effeminate. Somehow, these boys knew there was something different about him.

"Then one day, several of those boys cornered him in the locker room while he was getting ready to go to his next class after gym. He tried to fight them because he was scared. But I think now he was scared because he knew he would like what they were going to do him. You know how sometimes you just *know* something is going to happen, and exactly what that something is going to be?"

I nodded. Juan Carlos smiled.

"Those boys tied him up with their belts and shoved underwear in his mouth so he couldn't cry out. The leader slapped the boy on the ass, hard. Not because he thought the boy would like it, but as punishment. After a few minutes, this boy, he spit on the hole of the other and forced his way inside him. The boy screamed and screamed, but that punk was not going to stop. He fucked the boy like a girl. Until he came. After that, they all took turns on him. It was a little easier after the first one because his cum was like . . . how do you say? Lubrication."

I gulped as Juan Carlos continued to stare me down.

"When they were all done, they left him. The cleaning man found him."

"What . . . what happened then?"

"Nothing."

"What do you mean, nothing? He was raped!"

"Yes, but nothing happened because the boy was embarrassed. He would have been humiliated if he told anyone."

"But if he was raped . . ."

Juan Carlos shook his head as if I failed to understand. "It's true. He was raped. It's true he was embarrassed to be found that way, and humiliated because of what had been done. But there was one thing. The boy enjoyed it. While he was raped, he had an erection. And while the last punk fucked him, just before he came up his ass, the other boy came, too. Without touching himself."

"Oh my God!" I said, suddenly realizing. "It was you, wasn't it? You were the one who instigated it. You were the ring leader."

15

Juan Carlos remained silent. He sighed heavily and shook his head.

"No. I was . . . I was the one they . . ."

"Gang banged," I finished, now more aroused than ever.

"For many years after that, I tried to deny that I enjoyed getting fucked. Especially by force! I went out with lots of girls to hide it. Then, in college, there was a boy I fell in love with. I never told him how I felt. I was too scared of my feelings and afraid he would reject me."

"Then you came here."

"Yes. I became friends with the girl of the family that sponsored me. She was very popular and introduced me to all kinds of people. One night, we went to a party together. I got drunk and told her that I liked boys. She couldn't believe it. I think she didn't want to believe it because she started to like me. She asked if I'd ever had sex with a girl."

"Did you?"

"Oh, sure! Many times! But I had to concentrate on the day those boys took turns fucking me, coming inside me. It was the only way I could fuck a girl and come."

"So how did you wind up getting married?"

"I got her pregnant."

I sat stunned. "So . . . so you're a father, too?"

"Yes. I was trying to prove that I didn't like boys. But my entire life has been a lie because I don't like girls. I like boys. Well, maybe not boys. Men. I like men. And . . . I like you."

"Juan Carlos, I . . . I don't know what to say."

"Say you like me, too."

"Isn't it obvious?" I spread my legs and cupped my bulging crotch at him.

"Yes!" Juan Carlos sounded pleased. "I thought so, but I wasn't sure."

"Neither was I."

My cock was ready to burst. I looked at his Jockey-clad body. His cock was hard and jutting out in front of him, making a tent out of his white briefs. He smiled his innocent boy's smile and then he stepped toward me.

"Come! Get out of your clothes so I can see you naked!" He demanded.

I rapidly overcame my surprise and stood, stripping down to my underwear. We stood facing each other, dressed only in briefs and white socks.

"Oh, yes!" Juan Carlos bit his lower lip and looked at me with a wicked stare. He reached inside his Jockeys and hauled out a fat, cut eight-incher.

My mouth watered.

"Get on your knees. I want to watch you suck my fat cock. I want to see your lips stretched and your face turn red swallowing it to the balls. I want to see you play with yourself while you suck me off." Juan Carlos seemed to have lost all politeness. And I didn't need to be told twice.

And if Juan Carlos wanted to be in charge, who was I to complain?

I sank to the floor and reached for his cock. After all that time spent wondering what it looked like, and longing for it, I finally had it in my greedy hands and I wasn't planning on letting go until he begged for mercy.

I wrapped my fist around the base and pumped it. Juan Carlos threw his head back and moaned. I leaned forward, parted my lips, and let the tip of my tongue explore his piss slit. A drop of precum oozed out and trickled onto my taste buds. He tasted every bit as sweet as I imagined.

A frenzied hunger suddenly filled me and flowed through my veins. I kissed the tip of his cock and played with his balls while licking the entire length of his engorged shaft. Then, unable to stand it any longer, Juan Carlos grabbed the back of my head and forced me down on his meat. The tip pushed past my throat, making me gag, but I held my ground. Soon, my nose was buried in his blond pubic patch, his balls pressing against my chin. I inhaled deeply, his strong musky odor hitting me like an aphrodisiac. I moaned wantonly and pulled back on his meat, his shaft covered in spit, leaving only the tip in my mouth.

I leaned back on my haunches and Juan Carlos followed my moves, both of his hands holding on to my head. Standing up, he was now able to fuck my face with fervor. I prepared myself for the onslaught, relaxing my throat muscles, loving the way his strong hands held my head firmly in place for his cock pleasure.

My cock was drooling and it hurt pleasurably, trapped as it was in the confines of my briefs. I reached into the elastic and pulled it down past my balls. With my right fist firmly wrapped around the base of my cock, I started stroking.

Looking up, I stared into Juan Carlos' eyes as he looked down at his cock disappearing and reappearing. He muttered inaudible things in Spanish to me. I relished the workout he was giving my jaw, my sexy skull fucker pounding my face. I loved the feel of his balls as they swayed to and fro, slapping me on the chin.

It wasn't long before Juan Carlos began to breathe heavily. His balls drew up into his body and I knew I would soon have him shooting his load. I worked my throat muscles, squeezing down on his meat and throbbing cockhead. I wanted to milk him down to the very last drop.

Juan Carlos began to moan, his tone dropping lower, and gave a final thrust. He grunted and plunged his Spanish meat deep into my mouth just as I stopped jerking off. The first squirt fired and hit the back of my throat. I swallowed, struggling to keep his shaft buried, but I wanted to taste his seed. The hold he had on my head relaxed slightly as I pulled back. I opened my mouth and stuck my tongue out so as not to spill a single drop of his delicious nectar.

Two more spurts, thick, rich, and creamy, oozed onto my tongue. I wrapped my lips around the head of his shaft and kept my tongue just underneath the piss slit, savoring the bittersweet taste of his cum. I wrapped a fist around his meat, pumping and milking him for everything he had. I swallowed feverishly, as if he were my sustenance and I, a starving man. When the throbbing finally subsided, Juan Carlos pulled me up and thrust his tongue into my mouth.

"Oh, Johnny. You don't know how good that felt!"

"That was a big load!"

Juan Carlos shrugged. "It's been a while." He looked down, nodding at my still-jumping shaft. "You didn't jerk off."

19

I smiled back at him. "I was going to, but, I figured it would be a waste. I'd rather feel it sliding down your throat."

"You want me to suck your cock?" His smiled broadened. I nodded. He looked down at my hard prick again and slowly sank to his knees. He pulled my Jockeys down as he went and my cock sprang up, slapping against my stomach. "Hmmm. Very nice!" He took my cock in his hand and looked at it. He seemed to hesitate, then he looked up. "Just don't fuck my mouth, okay? I'll choke if you do. I'm not a very good cocksucker."

He opened his mouth and slipped his lips over the tip of my cock. I looked down and watched at how hot his lips looked as they spread, taking more and more of my shaft. He pulled back and I gasped as his teeth bite down on the fleshy, purple head. Slowly he worked his head back forth, nibbling along the way, until he had as much of my cock as he could take. Wrapping his fist around the last few inches, he pumped my spit-slick shaft.

I had been so close that it wasn't long before I came. I pulled out of his mouth and wrapped my fist around the base of my dick, pumping and squirting my load all over Juan Carlos' sweet, innocent face. He moaned as each spurt fell on his flesh, his mouth open and his long tongue circling. He smacked his lips, tongue lapping at what it could reach. I leaned over him and licked off the rest, feeding some to him. We sucked on each other's tongue until we could no longer taste the flavor of cum.

"Oh, man! That was great! But what am *I* going to do now?" He had a petulant look on his face. He leaned back and shook his hard cock at me.

Without responding, I stepped aside and draped my torso over the desk, grasping the end of it. After weeks of fantasizing, I was eager to feel him pump my ass full of come.

Juan Carlos stood, stroking the length of his hard cock. He rummaged through one of the cabinets beneath the counter next to the sink and pulled out a jug of cooking oil. "It's all I have."

I shrugged. "Go for it!"

Juan Carlos opened the jug and tipped some oil into the palm of his hand. He rubbed it over the length of his tool, making it shiny, then capped it and slammed the jug down on the counter. Walking back towards me, Juan Carlos then sat down in the chair I'd been sitting in. He grabbed his cock by the base and waved it at me.

"I have a better idea. Why don't we pretend I'm Santa Claus. Now, come sit on my lap and tell me what you want for Christmas."

I let go the desk and walked over to him. Turning my back on him, I then spread my legs, reaching between them to grab a hold of his oily meat. It throbbed in my hand and I squeezed, lowering myself until the tip was rubbing against my puckered, twitching asshole. I rubbed it against the rim of my anxious fuckhole.

Juan Carlos grabbed me by the waist and pulled me down on him. The lips of my asshole stretched and yielded to the thick helmet that was his head and it plopped inside me. I spasmed, as inch by agonizing inch, the entire length of his shaft ripped me open. The pain was rich and glorious, but I refused to get off.

He continued pulling me onto him, impaling me with the thick fucktool. I could feel the raw flesh around my asshole burning and stretching to accommodate the sudden intrusion. My body broke out into a sweat, but Juan Carlos didn't stop until he had all of his cock balls deep inside me.

"That's it, Johnny!" His voice was a whisper. "You have all of it up your ass." Juan Carlos wrapped his arms around my torso and kissed my sweaty back. "My dick feels so good up your ass. It's so tight!" He leaned back in the chair, and grabbed me by the waist. He then pushed me off his shaft until only the head remained firmly entrenched within me. Then he pulled me back onto his shaft and I moaned, sinking down with one slow plunge. Pure pleasure coursed through my veins.

"Oh, yeah!" I sighed, and began to rock. The oil heated up as I rode him faster and faster, slamming down on Juan Carlos as if I were fucking myself on a battering ram. "Oh, baby! Your cock feels so fuckin' good up my ass! It's so hot, so thick. Juan Carlos, I feel like I'm burning up!"

"Yeah, Johnny, I know. I'm on fire, too. Feels good, doesn't it? You like the way my fat cock feels up your tight ass?" I moaned and nodded.

Juan Carlos reached around with his right hand and grabbed my bouncing meat in his fist. It was still greasy with oil and he ran it over my dick. I pumped myself full of his juicy fuckstick while at the same time pumping my cock in his fist.

"Oh, Juan Carlos! I'm gonna come! I'm gonna . . . I . . . *I'm coming!*"

Juan Carlos reached around with his left hand and cupped it underneath the tip of my spurting dickhead. I shot my load into the palm of his hand and he raised it to my mouth as an offering. I stuck my tongue out and lapped it up.

While slurping up my own load, I continued impaling myself on Juan Carlos' shaft. Suddenly, he moaned and cried out as he shot his second load up my ass. I felt him throbbing inside me as his sperm bathed the walls of my fuckhole.

We sat there a moment. His cock slowly went limp inside me, our bodies glued together with our sweat. Finally, I stood and his cock slurped out of my asshole, wet and slimy.

We dressed in silence. When we were ready to leave, we turned to face each other. Juan Carlos smiled. "I'd like to have that drink you offered me earlier."

"You would?" He nodded. "What about your wife?"

He shrugged his shoulders. "She can buy her own drink!"

I smirked and shook my head. "Then let's go to my place instead. We'll be more comfortable there. Besides . . ."

Juan Carlos cocked his head and waited for me to finish. But I left him hanging. I grinned and walked past him. He reached out for my arm.

"Wait a minute! Don't walk away like that! Finish what you started."

I turned around, hands in my pockets and threw my head back to glare at him. "I'm planning on doing just that, Juan Carlos. Now, you coming home with me or what?" I walked out into the corridor and started for the elevators. I could hear him behind me.

"Wait up! C'mon, man. At least let me lock up?"

I slowed my gait, hearing the keys rattling on the ring. He gave the door a good solid shove to make sure it had locked, then trotted behind me.

I couldn't wait to get home and fuck *him*!

# Baby Doll

Frank Cox was glad the week was almost over. It had been particularly stressful, what with end-of-quarter analysis reports, budget cuts looming on the horizon, and key people on his staff away on vacation.

He looked at the clock on his desk. *Only two hours to go!*

Frank couldn't wait to go out later that night and cruise the bars. In fact he'd been looking forward to it all week. He was planning on picking up some rough, sweaty number and fuck until they both dropped. He needed some relief and it was the only he knew how to get it.

Putting aside all thoughts of fucking himself into oblivion, Frank brought his attention back to the project at hand and tackled it with new- found fervor.

At the end of the day, after a stressful drive home during rush hour, Frank was about ready to collapse. He ignored his usual routine of punching the answering machine for messages while firing up the computer to check for e-mail. Instead, Frank stripped on his way to the bedroom, then flung himself on the bed for a nap. He was asleep within minutes.

When he awakened several hours later, Frank was famished. He fixed himself a tossed salad, scoffed it down, then turned on his Bose stereo. While his favorite techno music filtered through the speakers and wafted through the apartment, Frank danced about, preparing for a night of carousing and debauchery.

After a hot shower, he brushed his teeth and stood before the oversized mirror that covered nearly the entire wall of his bedroom. He scrutinized the image reflected before him; full, red lips that were just made for kissing and cock-sucking; dark brown eyes that would make any puppy admirer melt; a smooth, tight body that was admired by every one, every time he went out; and a fat, decent length of meat lolling against his right leg that swelled to nearly eight inches of uncut beef.

Bagging himself a big-dicked stud to bring home was a sure thing. He felt it in his bones. A sexy, crooked smile broke across his face as the confidence surged within him, alongside his desire.

*Shit! I'm so fucking horny right now! Maybe I'll just stay home and fuck my real doll!*

But no. His doll, no matter how realistic, simply would not do. Frank needed real flesh and blood. A hard, throbbing, grunting, fucking machine pounding him to oblivion. Frank tugged on his cock and stroked it lightly, then turned away from the mirror to get dressed.

Socks, a pair of faded, black 501s, black leather boots and a sheer, black tank top that showed off his smooth, well-defined chest. He wore nothing under his jeans but a cockring. The cold metal made his thick, uncut cock jut out further and the semi-turgid meat perfectly outlined against his jeans made his building desire grow to a steamy, bubbling boil.

*Fuck! Definitely no doll for me tonight. I need me some REAL cock!*

With his thick, straight, dark blond hair slightly mussed up on purpose, Frank left his apartment and made his way outside.

On the street, Frank got many admiring stares; one from a really cute kid he'd seen around the neighborhood. Frank looked at the kid's face as he cruised by slowly; he looked to be about 19 or 20; but his eyes spoke of an age that far exceeded his physical body.

Frank scanned the boy's body, his eyes coming to rest at the boy's crotch, then admiring his round, very fuckable buns. He briefly thought of taking the boy back home with him, but suddenly decided against it.

*No, I don't want a boy tonight. I need a Man! A hot, raunchy, sweaty mother fucker to fuck the shit outta me!*

Frank smiled at the kid, nodded, and continued past him.

A few blocks away, Frank walked into one of his favorite bars, *The Chocolate Factory*. He thought perhaps he would enjoy picking up a big, rough black man. He climbed up on one of the stools.

"Hiya, Frankie!" The bartender greeted in a gruff voice. He was a big, black man built like a football player.

"Hi, Toby." Frank smiled. "How's it hangin'?"

"Wanna see for yourself?" The bartender smiled, pulling away from the counter. He exposed an achingly huge mound in worn jeans that looked as if they would unravel at the slightest touch.

"Fuck! That's hot, Toby!" Frank grinned and shot Toby a lewd grin.

"So's your hot ass!" Toby flashed him a white, toothy grin.

Frank licked his lips at Toby and thought of his monster cock, remembering the night he had gone home with him.

Toby had wanted to fuck Frank, but he'd taken one look at the chocolate brown fuck stick and was instantly frightened. Eventually, Toby persuaded Frank to roll over on his stomach, his legs spread wide. Toby had slicked up Frank's hole with his tongue for nearly half an hour, thrusting the fat, pink thing into the very tight, very tense asshole. After much spit and a lot of Vaseline, Toby had managed to probe Frank's butt with his thick, long, black shaft. He had cried out when Toby's fat, pink cockhead plopped inside his underused asshole. And although he had protested, Toby ignored him, knowing full well Frank would enjoy his huge meat up his tight, white ass once the entire length was inside him.

When Toby had almost half of his prick inside him, Frank had begun to moan and sigh, his own cock at half mast. He had backed up against Toby's groin, impaling himself suddenly on the black spear penetrating his rectum. His orgasm that night had been the most violent Frank had ever experienced. Even when Toby shot his load inside Frank, he had felt every single spurt of cum bathing his rectal sleeve.

It had certainly been the best fuck he'd ever had and he was glad Toby had coaxed him into getting fucked that night.

His memory triggered a hard-on, and Frank felt his cock snaking further down his pants leg.

"So what'll it be, Frankie?"

"A Black Russian."

"Coming right up, baby doll!" Toby grinned at Frank.

While Toby fixed his drink, Frank looked around. "Slow night, huh?" He looked back at Toby as he served his drink.

"Yeah. It's pretty slow. Usually, by now, all the brothers are standing around shoulder to shoulder, just waiting for their juices to be drained or their holes to be plucked. But not tonight. Don't know what's happening! It's been this way for a coupla weeks, now."

"You're kidding?" Frank said disappointedly.

"Nope." Toby shook his head. Then he shot Frank a wry, admiring smile. "So, what you been up to my man?"

"Oh, this and that. Busy working mostly." Frank shrugged.

A few men bustled in and sat down at the end of the bar.

"Excuse me, Frankie." Toby turned and left to serve the other patrons. Frank sat alone with his Black

Russian. He drank it quickly, suddenly realizing he might not get what he was looking for.

He slammed the glass down on the counter and waved at Toby.

"Leaving so soon?" Toby called out.

"Yeah! I'm in search of a man who obviously isn't here tonight."

Toby nodded, looking somewhat disappointed. For a moment, Frank almost took pity on him; he knew Toby had liked him more than he let on. But it wasn't what Frank was looking for that night. And although the thought of Toby's cock burrowing up his tight, itchy hole appealed to him, Frank wanted something new; something different. Something he'd not had before.

The next few bars Frank went to produced the same results. They were either not as full as they normally were, or the men he encountered were simply not worth Frank's effort.

By the time he stepped into the fourth bar, it was nearing two in the morning. Frank was desperate and drunk. He was practically feverish with desire as he walked the streets with a massive hard-on. He would stroke it as he walked past a man he found arousing, in the hopes of enticing them to come home with him.

To no avail.

Burning with lust, Frank decided to head for the baths. Halfway there, he changed his mind. Sometimes the baths scared him; you never knew what you were going to find there. And on a night like the one he was having, every instinct in his body told him he would find nothing but trolls.

Near his apartment, the lights at the *End-Up* beckoned. On a whim, Frank decided to have one final drink. If he didn't find anyone there, he would just call it quits and go home.

Inside, Frank sidled up to a stool and ordered another Black Russian. Waiting for his drink, he took in the lack of fuckable men. Disappointed that his anticipated evening was a bust, Frank thought once again about Baby. Of course, it wasn't the same as fucking a real guy, but the manufacturer had called him the perfect lover. It's name was Winston, but Frank dubbed him Baby Doll; always willing, always ready.

"Baby Doll," Frank whispered out loud, smiling at the thought. How foolish he had been. He should have followed his instinct and stayed home instead of wasting time looking for a real man.

"Fuck it!" Frank blurted. He downed his drink in just a few swigs, slammed the glass down on the counter and rushed out of the bar. He had a doll waiting for him at home!

His hole burning with desire, his balls nearly twice their normal size and swollen with unspilled cum, Frank's cock felt as if it was about to burst by the time he got home. Frank massaged his aching balls as he walked into his apartment and shut the door behind him.

Kicking off his shoes, Frank peeled the socks from his feet as he made his way to the bedroom. He pulled the tank top over his head as he walked to the closet and flung the short drunkenly away from him. It landed on a lamp shade. He tugged at his belt, then undid the buttons of his 501s. With great difficulty,

Frank slid his jeans down his hips. His stiff, aching prick sprang up and slapped against his belly.

The tip of his cock peeked out through the folds of foreskin and Frank grabbed it between thumb and forefinger. He peeled the skin back, exposing the wide, leaking piss slit and rubbed the oozing pre-cum with his thumb over the fat, purple cockhead. He closed his eyes, threw his head back slightly and sighed deeply.

Frank released his cock and threw open the closet door. He pushed the clothes aside in a wide gesture. Standing there before him, at the back of his closet, was Baby Doll. His arms were up, open and waiting, but his eyes almost seemed to express disappointment at being locked away.

Frank looked at him and smiled meekly.

"I'm sorry, Baby. I should have . . . well, never mind. Look's like it's just you and me, kid!" Fueled by his drunken stupor, Frank grabbed the life-sized, life-like rubber doll, pulled him out of the closet and flung him on the bed.

Baby was a custom rubber doll that Frank had ordered over the internet, made according to Frank's carefully detailed request list. Several months later, it had been shipped in a crate that might have contained a coffin inside it.

His skin was life-like, though somewhat cold since Frank wasn't about to waste time submerging him in a bathtub filled with warm water.

The dolls hair, almost as realistic as human hair, was coarse to the touch.

Frank kissed the dolls open, yielding mouth. It was a perfect fit for Frank's hardened, throbbing cock. A mechanism at the back of the doll's head, barely detectable, allowed him to make Baby's mouth a bit more snug. And his arms, smooth but firm and sculpted, were bent at the elbow as if to welcome his lover home with an embrace. The perfect man; the perfect lover. Always there, always willing, and always able.

"And you never talk back, do you, Baby?"

Frank lay down on top of Baby, rubbing his body all over the soft, fleshy rubber, feeling his own erection as it stiffened even more against Baby's permanent boner. Frank moaned.

"That's what's so good about you, Baby. You can always keep your dick hard."

Baby just stared off into space.

Frank looked down between the dolls legs, at the realistic cock; seven inches long, four inches thick. He came with two attachments which the owner simply slipped over the doll's permanent one; the first one measured nine inches in length, six thick inches; the second, for those nights when Frank wanted just a little more, was thirteen inches in length and nearly eight inches around.

Frank moved down over Baby's latex skin and clamped his mouth over the rubber cock. He worked on it until it was slippery from his own spit, working the doll's dick into the back of his throat. After a while, Frank turned around, straddling Baby's head so that he was in a 69 position.

While he continued sucking on Baby's cock, Frank began force feeding Baby his own shaft until it was balls deep inside Baby's oral opening. Then he fucked his face with a frenzy while he downed Baby's rubber prick greedily; he pumped his cock hard into the doll's mouth, feeling his balls slap against Baby's forehead.

"Okay, Baby!" Frank pulled off the doll's cock and jumped out of bed. Walking to his dresser, Frank grabbed the half-empty jar of lube and came back to his doll. "I'm gonna sit on your cock now and fuck myself with your hard rubber tool!" He pulled the lid off the jar and dipped his fingers into the gooey mess inside. He fingered the mess into his hole while clamping his teeth over the doll's nipples.

Frank bit down as if they were made of real flesh; his tongue would not have known the difference in the dark. His ears, however, missed the sharp intake of breath a real man would have made. But in a way the doll was better. Frank could suck, bite, and pull on Baby's nipples as hard as he wanted to and not worry about hurting him.

By now, Frank was totally turned on to the idea of making it with his Baby Doll; the doll that was always there when he needed it. The doll that was always in the mood; the doll that would always let him fuck it's mouth or it's ass, and never ever say no to Frank.

*How much better than a real man you are, Baby!*

Frank now shoved two of his own lubed fingers up his ass and greased up his hole, readying himself for Baby's cock.

"Okay, Baby! Let's DO it!"

Frank straddled the doll, spread his buns apart, then slowly brought his hole to the tip of Baby's steel-hard, rubber prick. He teased himself with the doll's cock, rubbing himself back and forth on the realistic cockhead, trying to make his own pleasure last longer.

Then Frank sank down, allowing his asshole to clench around the tip of Baby's cock. He moaned as Baby's stiffness stretched his quivering hole. He sank down further, taking another couple of inches up his ass. Frank sighed, rolling his head around with his eyes closed. He had forgotten that he was making it with a doll. He had what he wanted now; a good, hard prick up his ass.

Sinking down even further, Frank sighed deeply and began stroking his own throbbing cock as he impaled himself on the full length of Baby's shaft.

"Oh, yeah!" Frank moaned. "Now I'm gonna fuck myself with your hard rubber tool!" Slowly, Frank started riding the doll's dick, rising up, then sinking. He moaned every time the tip of Baby's cock hit his prostate and knew that if he didn't stop stroking his cock, he would soon shoot a load all over Baby's chest. But Frank Cox didn't want to come yet.

He raised himself up off of Baby's rubber prick, and turned the doll over. He stared at his round, bubble butt.

*If I didn't know it was a doll, I'd swear it was real!*

Frank dipped his fingers into the jar of lube again and greased his pulsating shaft. Thrusting his middle finger into the doll's asshole, Frank relished in the sudden tightness. Here the rubber was soft, yet somehow firm, conforming and yielding without resistance to Franks probing finger.

Frank poised himself over the prone doll. Holding himself up on one hand, Frank grabbed the base of his throbbing fuckstick, aiming the tip at Baby's fuckhole. He pushed forward and Frank felt the doll's pliant ass open to swallow the throbbing head of his cock.

Slowly, as if fucking a virgin, Frank continued to sink the length of his cock into Baby. When he was buried balls deep within the confines of the doll, Frank pulled out and plunged again. Clenching his teeth and trying to hold back a heavy, creamy load, he fucked the doll's ass with a fury. He did push-ups into Baby's ass, thrusting in and out, pumping him full of hard meat.

Then, just as he was about to come, Frank pulled out. He wrapped his fingers around the base of his shaft and squeezed down hard. By sheer force of will, Frank held back. He wanted to come while impaled on Baby's biggest attachment; the thirteen incher!

Frank had been avoiding using the largest attachment since Baby was shipped to him. He had wanted to, several times, but didn't know if his ass could take it.

*But tonight I want it! Even if it rips my hole apart!*

Frank lay down next to Baby while he lit a joint. He sucked the acrid smoke into his lungs and felt his body relaxing even more. Reaching over to the nightstand on the right side of the bed, Frank opened the top drawer. Inside were some fuck books for late night reading, some leather and metal cockrings, handcuffs; and Baby's attachments.

Frank pulled out the biggest one and held it in his hand. He stared at the huge piss slit, admiring the sheer size and weight of the enormous rubber dong riddled with realistic veins. They looked as if they were pulsating. Frank's mouth watered. He licked his lips.

*Fuck! This thing sure is huge!*

And for a brief moment, he doubted whether or not he could take it. But he had made up his mind. Putting out the joint in the ashtray, Frank turned to Baby, slipped the monstrous hose over his permanent cock and made sure it was firmly in place. He cupped Baby's huge, life-like balls and gave them a firm squeeze. Warm liquid shot out through Baby's piss slit and he knew the alignment was perfect.

"Sure wish that was real, Baby!" Frank muttered out loud, almost regretfully.

In addition to the attachments, Baby had come with the refillable balls option. Inside, a thin, bendable tube ran from the doll's nut sac to the tip of his cock. The balls were filled with any liquid the owner desired. A small hole with a plug, like on a water gun, kept the liquid from spilling.

Frank had ordered tubes of flavored jellies that when mixed with water, these jellies turned into a syrup. He'd ordered banana and pineapple. Baby's balls were now filled with pineapple.

Dipping his fingers once more into the jar of lube, Frank slowly and deliberately greased up the huge member before him. His puckered rosebud twitched and throbbed and ached with anticipation. The huge monster cock attachment looked even more obscene, even more realistic not that it was all greased up.

Frank looked down at the monster cock, all slick and shiny and felt his butthole twitch and pucker. His body shivered, and Frank would have sworn he could feel Baby's cock pulsing and throbbing in his practiced hand.

He dipped his fingers into the jar again, then greased up his still-lubed, already fucked manhole. He massaged his prostate, pushing his fingers deeper and deeper. He groaned as he slid first one, then two and, finally, three fingers in and out of his own asshole.

Inspired by the realistic, colossal meat before him, Frank decided to go whole hog and shoved yet another finger up his own ass. With four fingers up his chute, Frank was nearly delirious. Between the joint and the booze, the endorphins running through his body made him feel like he was on a real trippy high.

"Oh, Baby! I'm ready for you now! I'm *sooooo* fucking ready!" Frank moaned and sighed. The doll stared up at the ceiling, his lips almost in a teasing smile.

Frank straddled the doll and rubbed his finger-fucked asshole over the fat tip of Baby's attachment. Thinking of the searing, sharp pain that would shoot through his body and the wonderful pleasure-pain that would follow, Frank sat down on the huge, thick cock. His asshole stretched wider than it had ever done before and he groaned.

There was discomfort he might have called pain if he had not been so stoned and drunk, yet Frank pushed himself further. He pushed out with his rectum as if he were taking a shit, and quite suddenly, the bulbous cockhead plopped into Frank's sore, throbbing asshole. He gave a sharp cry as the pain stabbed at his body and forced himself to relax.

*C'mon, fucker! Open up! Let that rubber prick slip inside you!*

Frank closed his eyes, bit his lower lip against the pain and tried to imagine his ass lips stretching wider. At the same time, he pushed down, pushing out with his rectum. He sighed as he slid down further and a couple of rubber inches bore through him.

Pausing long enough to reach into the open drawer, Frank pulled out a bottle of poppers, uncapped it, and took a large hit. The blood pounded his head, filled his veins and he nearly swooned from the efforts of trying to breath. The only thing that mattered was the connection between his sphincter and the monster cock he was determined to take all the way down to the balls.

With a gasp, Frank pushed himself down further, imagining the entire length of rubber deep inside his bowels.

It took him nearly fifteen minutes but, eventually, Frank managed to take all of the thick, near life-like rubber. He gave a final grunt of perverse satisfaction as he slammed down on the last remaining inch of Baby's meat. With the thirteen inch monster cock firmly entrenched up his wide opened manhole, Frank felt the insides of his rectal sleeve burn as his bowels accustomed to the intrusion. His entire rectum cried out from a mixture of shock and pleasureable pain as he raggedly gulped down air.

Frank reached between his legs and felt his asshole. His eyes flung open and his mouth went slack as sudden tears of joy poured forth. He had never been fucked by anything so huge! And he had never felt such immense ecstasy; it was almost as if he were having a religious experience.

With Baby's cock firmly inside him, Frank waited a few moments before moving. He couldn't believe he had taken the whole thing; he felt so full! The pressure inside him was strong and his entire body seemed to throb. Frank reached behind him and cupped Baby's balls. He squeezed and felt the syrup squirt his insides. Then, as if that had been the inspiration he needed,

Frank reached for his own limp cock and stroked it until he got hard. Then he went to work.

He planted the bottoms of his feet firmly on either side of Baby and lifted himself up. The thick root burned the tender insides of his rectal sleeve; but he didn't care. Frank continued lifting himself until the only thing that remained inside him was the incredibly fat tip of Baby's cock. Then he lowered himself back down onto it, slowly so as to feel every agonizing inch of the hot, rubber tool.

Frank was beyond ecstasy; he was delirious. He sighed deeply and loudly as he fucked himself on the doll's monster shaft. It felt too good, and too real for him to hold back any longer. He pounded his ass up and down on the monstrous rubber cock. With his eyes closed, Frank rode Baby's prick, his own cock slapping against Baby's groin as he sank down to the hilt. He pinched his own nipples, feeling his body burn and tremble from the fuck fever that possessed him when he was deeply penetrated.

"Oh, FUCK!" Frank wailed. He slammed himself down on Baby's cock again and again. "I'm gonna do it, Baby! I'm gonna cum! Baby! Oohhhhhhh!"

Pinching his own nipples and ramming himself onto Baby's cock, Frank felt the first tremor shake him to the very core. He wailed as his cock throbbed and finally burst, without touching himself. And yet he continued to slam himself down and wiggle his ass from side to side.

With his eyes still closed, Frank reached behind him and squeezed on Baby's balls while he came, his asshole clenching and spasming around the doll's huge rubber tool. He felt the thick juice as it splattered against the walls of his fuckhole and moaned.

It seemed to Frank his orgasm was nearly eternal. He kept his eyes closed as long as he could and when the throbbing inside his body started to abate, he opened them. The heavy load he had stored up all week had sprayed out almost in a straight line; the first squirt had shot out like a bullet, spraying thick fuckjuice on Baby's chin, a second had landed between the valley of his well-defined pecs, and the rest had pooled in and around Baby's belly button.

Unable to stand the pressure against his bladder any longer, Frank raised himself up and felt the walls of his chute cling to the rubber cock, ever so slowly releasing as he pushed out.

Frank stared at the huge cock he had just fucked himself with. He wrapped his lips around the tip of Baby's cockhead while his hole clenched shut, then opened, clamped then opened, eventually relaxing itself to a dull, pulsating throb.

Frank squeezed the doll's syrup-filled balls a few times and the warm juice hit the back of his throat. He pulled away, sat up and swallowed Baby's pineapple-flavored load.

His entire body wracked with pleasure, Frank then lay down quietly next to the doll, realizing for the first time that dawn was rapidly approaching. Frank reached between his legs and with gentle strokes of his fingertips, felt his raw, abused fuckhole; a tremendous heat emanated from deep within him. The fingers slipped in easily and a sense of contentment flowed through Frank.

He felt his eyelids begin to droop and suddenly felt the week catch up to him. He was dead tired. Pulling the fingers out from his well-used manhole, Frank rolled over onto his stomach. He draped an arm over Baby's chest, closed his eyes, and finally fell asleep.

Sleeping, Frank smiled. And so, too, did his Baby Doll.

# Laundry Room Fuck

*Today is going to be a special day!* I thought as I awakened.

A special day indeed. Later that morning I would no longer be a virgin. The very thought of what was to come got my dick hard. I stroked it a few times, then stopped. As much as I wanted to shoot a hot load of young, creamy cum all over my belly, I didn't want to waste it.

I forced myself to jump out of bed and start my day. I had a lot to before Roy came over, before I gave myself to him. I thought back to the day I first met him.

I had been on my way to school. The platform was normally crowded during rush hour. That morning, however, it had been more crowded than usual. There had been a delay on the D line.

When the train finally pulled into the station, it was already packed. I shoved my way in and found myself wedged between the door behind me, and a well-built blonde standing before me dressed in a navy blue, pin-striped suit, crisp white shirt and a bright red tie.

The doors rattled closed and I was pressed even tighter against him. As the train began to move, the people swayed back and forth. With nothing to hold onto, I lurched toward him. He looked up from his Wall Street Journal, an annoyed look in his eye.

"Excuse me. I'm sorry!" I apologized, looking up at him.

"S'okay." He mumbled and went back to reading his paper.

As the train barreled along it's way, I reached into my back pocket to pull out the paperback I had to read for my English Lit class; Homer's *Odyssey*. I got lost in the story and it was a while before I noticed the pressure against my groin. I looked down to see what it was and felt myself blush. I tried to focus but wound up rereading the same line several times before giving up.

I looked up from my book and caught the blonde man glancing down at me over the top of his paper. For a moment, our eyes held. The red creeping up my neck and face must have been as deep as his scarlet tie.

My own cock had stiffened at the feel of his burgeoning meat pressing against me, our crotches rubbing together as the train swayed. I had to bite my lower lip to keep from moaning. I nearly swooned when the train lurched wildly through a curve, throwing the man against me. He pinned me to the door beneath his weight.

"Sorry." His voice was deep and rumbly. "My turn to excuse myself."

I cleared my throat. "It's . . . s'okay." I croaked and looked up at him.

"I guess I wasn't meant to read the paper today." He smiled.

"I guess I wasn't meant to read either." I closed my book and shoved it back into my pocket.

"The Odyssey, huh?" He folded his paper and tucked it underneath his right arm. "I read that my senior year in college, a few years back. You a senior?"

"Freshman."

"Freshman?" A grin spread across the blonde man's face. "Really? What are you . . . all of . . . 19?"

"18." I swallowed nervously. He nodded appreciatively as his right hand worked its way to my crotch, rubbing and stroking me.

As packed as the train was, somehow, even more people managed to get on. The man kept looking into my eyes, cupping my stiff, throbbing cock. He let it go for just a moment, reached for my hand and placed it on his own hard mound. I groped and squeezed his cock as he thrust his hips forward, slow and hard.

At one point he leaned forward and whispered into my ear. "I feel like I could cum just like this." I looked up at him and simply nodded. He smiled down at me.

He leaned forward again. "But I want to cum with you."

I looked around nervously, as if someone might have heard. But, of course, no one had. Everyone was busy sleeping on their feet, or staring furiously at some invisible spot over someone's head, too angry at the delay and the crowded conditions to be aware of their surroundings. I didn't know what to say to him.

"I . . ." I looked around nervously then looked back up at him. He was looking down at me with an amused look and a raised eyebrow. I stepped on my tip toes and leaned into him.

"I've never done this before," I whispered into his ear.

"Me either." The blonde promised with a beguiling grin.

"In fact . . . I'm . . . a virgin."

"Really?" The man cocked his head to one side, his eyebrow arching even more invitingly. I nodded. He removed his hand from my crotch and I suddenly felt it cupping my left cheek. I nearly came on the spot. I closed my eyes and bit my lower lip, hoping no one was watching or that no one knew what was happening. But in a way, that was part of the excitement.

The train pulled into the next station and the doors suddenly flew open. He removed his hand abruptly just as someone rudely shoved up against me. As the train started to move again, I suddenly felt a hardness press against my backside; it was more than I could bare. I didn't know what it was and I didn't care.

The juices inside my young cock and balls had been flowing for a while and, without warning, a moan escaped my lips before I could stifle it. I came without touching myself, the sudden gush of warmth adding to my embarrassment. My body burned as if I had a fever as several people turned to see what had happened.

A man behind me chuckled softly, his bulge continuing to grow and press against me; the blonde before me sighed. He reached into his jacket pocket and pulled out two cards and a pen as the train pulled into the last stop in Brooklyn.

"Quick, what's your number?" He jotted it down and stuffed the card into his shirt pocket. "Here!" He handed the other card to me and when the doors opened, he stepped out in a sudden flow of human bodies.

Jostled and tossed like a twig in a river, I grabbed a hold of the bar in the center of the car. I turned and looked for the blonde man, but he was gone; lost in a frenzied blur of subway riders.

As new passengers boarded, I looked to see the man who had pressed his erection against my backside, making me cum. A tall, dark black man stared back at me with a lecherous look on his face. He licked his lips lewdly, oblivious to the crowd around us. I looked down at the obscenely huge bulge between his legs and felt my own cock begin to harden again as he pressed down at the base of his groin. I watched, mesmerized, as the thick slab of black tubesteak snaked down his sweat pants and swelled, a growing wet spot spreading at the tip.

My knees turned to rubber and I took a step toward him. Then I stopped. A woman sitting nearby clicked her tongue in disgust. I turned away, feeling the heat rising within me. I wanted to die. Instead, I pulled the book from my pocket and buried my face in it.

Nearly two months had gone by after that incident. Unsure of proper protocol, I waited for Roy to call; but he never did. I thought perhaps he had lost my number, so, late one evening, I finally called.

"Roy?" I spoke softly when he picked up the phone. I could hear the sound of a television in the background.

"Yeah?" His voice was suspicious. Now I could hear the sound of little kid voices growing louder.

"Um, I'm the guy you met on the D train," I explained.

"Oh! Yeahhhh. That's right! How's it going?" His voice warmed up quite suddenly, then changed again when I heard a woman's voice in the background asking who called.

"I'm . . . okay," I replied, though I wasn't sure he had heard. It sounded as if he had muffled the mouthpiece. I heard him mutter something but I couldn't quite make out.

"I was . . . um, just wondering how you were?"

"Listen, this really isn't a good time," Roy explained.

"I was looking forward to hearing from you."

A moment of silence.

"Listen, kid," Roy spoke again, his voice lower as if not to be heard. "I'm glad you called. I really am. I just . . . can't talk right now. You free on Monday?"

"Yeah. It's a school holiday."

"Good. Why don't we hook up then? Can you host?"

"Oh," was the only response I could manage. I felt as if I had been wounded. We fell silent a moment.

"Listen, kid. I'm really sorry. I shoulda told you. I thought you were gonna call me that night. I was alone for a few days and I thought . . . you still there?"

"Yeah," I sighed heavily.

"I'll make it up to you. I promise. You have no idea what I'm capable of. The things I can make you feel."

And just like that, I allowed myself to move past his baggage.

We agreed on a time and the memory of that train ride suddenly seemed quite real again. Before we hung up, Roy's voice dropped even lower, to an almost seductive whisper. "Tell me something, kid. You really a virgin?"

"Kinda."

"You either are or you aren't."

"Does getting jerked off count?"

"That depends. Want to tell me about it?"

"It was another boy. When I was in high school."

"Is that right? Who was it?"

"A jock I tutored in my literature class. We just got kinda close one day when I was at his house. He started talking about sex."

"What about it?"

"I don't remember, really. I was too nervous! All I remember was that I was sitting on his bed and he was on a chair at his desk by the bed. Our feet were touching and the next thing I knew he was rubbing himself. Neither one of us said anything so I started doing the same. And then, without realizing it, we were both pulling our zippers down."

"Then what happened?" Roy pressed me for more details.

"We started jerking off together."

"And? Did you fuck each other?"

"No," I replied. Roy sounded disappointed.

"Did you at least blow him? Did he blow you?"

"Uh, no. His father came home then."

"Whoa! Fucking awesome! Did his father walk in on you?" By the huskiness in Roy's voice I knew he was aroused.

"No. He just zipped himself up, smacked me upside the head and called me a cocksucker. I felt like such a . . . pervert!"

"But you liked it right?" I nodded as if he could see me. He was silent a moment. "So, you think you're a good cocksucker?"

"I don't know."

"We'll find out Monday, won't we?"

All of a sudden his voice grew louder. He said he would see me at work tomorrow, then hung up. I could only assume that his wife had walked back into the room.

Monday finally arrived. After breakfast I whipped through my small apartment in a cleaning frenzy, then took a couple loads of dirty wash to the laundry room in the basement. Back upstairs to my apartment, I cleaned myself out, showered, then dressed. I was to meet Roy at the train station near my place.

I waited for him near the token booth. With every train that whooshed into the station, my heart skipped a beat. My cock stirred and my cherry rosebud puckered with anticipation. I couldn't wait for Roy to pop my cherry! Anxiously, I scanned the faces as people walked by, but no Roy. Fifteen minutes went by, then half an hour. I was getting annoyed.

"I'll give him 15 more minutes!" I mumbled to myself, went outside, and sat down on a bench just outside the station.

As I sat, I heard a lewd chuckle that was oddly and disturbingly familiar. I looked up and was startled to see the big, black man from the subway, the day I met Roy; the man that made me cum when he rubbed his hard cock against my ass. He walked slowly by as he exited the train station, a smile on his face. He wore mirrored sunglasses so I couldn't see his eyes, but I knew he had seen me. His brown skin was dark and shiny with sweat; I could smell him as he walked past. I hadn't noticed his build that day on the train; I had been too busy staring at the bulge in his pants.

He was solid, like a football player, with wide shoulders and massive thighs. He wore a white, sleeveless tee-shirt, red terry cloth shorts and a pair of Adidas running shoes with no socks. I drank in the sight of him then looked up at his face. His large, pink tongue licked his thick lips.

I glanced down at his crotch; the thick tube of flesh lay resting against his left thigh. I could see the length of it clearly; it had to be about five inches in length; and it was still limp!

I remembered the delicious sight of his hard on two months ago and licked my lips without even realizing it. The memory made me wonder how big the thing was when fully hard and my body tingled at the thought.

My balls contracted and my soft dick began to stir as I thought of the black man's soft dick in my warm, moist mouth. I wanted to cup his balls and bathe his big black dick with my wet tongue. I wanted to feel it harden in my throat, the tip of it making me gag. I wondered if I would ever be able to suck something that large and take it all down my throat.

As the big black man walked by, my eyes came to rest on his large, beefy bubble butt. It jiggled inside his shorts and my tongue nearly wagged. How I would have loved to bury my face in it.

He stopped suddenly and turned around, hands on his hips, waiting to see what I would do. Scared and nervous, I looked away. But I couldn't resist and just had to look back at him. He stood there and I merely stared at him, or rather, I stared at his crotch.

After a moment, however, he realized that my fear was too great. The grin on his face grew lop-sided, bright white teeth flashed at me and I wondered what they would feel like as he bit down on my nipples. Suddenly, he flipped me the bird, turned around and walked away. I watched him disappear as he turned the corner, and I could have kicked myself.

I felt oddly disappointed as I stood up and strolled over to the newspaper stand. There, I bought a roll of breath mints and popped one in my mouth. I went back to the bench and sat down again as another train rushed into the station; no Roy.

I popped another mint, lamenting over my inability to lose my virginity, when out of the corner of my eyes, I saw the big, black man again. I swallowed nervously, unable to move, all of a sudden frightened by the prospect that I could lose my virginity to the big dicked black man and now Roy, as I had originally planned.

Every nerve in my body told me to run, to get as far away as I could. Instead, my eyes slid slowly down to his crotch; his dick had grown longer, though still not fully hard. The thick head of his cock threatened to poke out from underneath the shorts. I looked back up at his face, but there was no lewd grin, no smile. The determined, mean look on his face frightened me into action.

Forgetting all about Roy, I got up from the bench and started walking away. My heart beat a little faster and I increased my gait when I saw his stride lengthen.

At the corner, I turned and sprinted. Behind me, a bottle cap scurried across the pavement and I knew he was catching up. Quickly, I dodged into a candy store, still about a block away from home, and pretended to survey the array of candy before me. I turned at the lip-smacking sounds near my ear and froze. He stood directly before me, a shit-eating grin on his face. I looked down at his crotch, now close enough to touch. He didn't even bother to hide his now stiff prick.

My body broke out in a frantic sweat and I stepped past him, my left hand grazing his erection. I moaned from fear and excitement, no longer caring if anyone saw, no longer concerned that he might be toying with me.

"Sorry!" I nearly knocked an old woman down as I ran out of the candy store.

I could still feel the man's eyes on me. All of a sudden, my round, virgin ass felt quite vulnerable. I had gone beyond fear and, for some reason I couldn't explain, now felt as if caught in a nightmare. And yet, the stiff bulge between my legs laughed at my fear, mocking my desire.

*Is this how it was going to be? Was I going to lose my virginity to some big black man whose name I don't even know?*

I ran across the street and turned another corner. In the distance, was the building where I lived. I looked over my shoulder. The black man wasn't far behind. His long legs shortened the distance between us and his wicked grin made me cringe.

And yet the sight of his bobbing dick made me drool.

I got to the front of my building, pushed the door open and quickly ducked inside, silently giving a prayer of thanks to whomever had left it unlocked.

Within the reasonable safety of the lobby, I slammed the glass door shut. I dashed across the marble tile, sprinted up the steps and turned right, towards the elevator.

Out of his sight, I stood with my back against the wall, feeling like a spy while I waited for my heart to stop tripping in my chest. Then I heard the door being pushed, as if someone were trying to force it open. It rattled a few times, echoing throughout the lobby, and then it stopped.

I waited a moment.

With my heart still pounding in my head, I swallowed hard and took a peak.

The black man stood across the street, legs spread, arms dangling at his sides. I looked at his face, at the mirrored sunglasses. A malicious sneer spread across his lips as he stared back at me, intimidating me into opening the door. I didn't know what I was more scared of; that he was so big, black and mean-looking or my desire for that huge piece of meat. I looked down at his crotch as if the answer where there. I licked my lips and realized that it was.

I took a step toward the door, then watched in amazement as he reached down and freed his dick from his shorts. It bobbed in the air, shiny and black.

He grinned slowly as he grabbed it by the base between thumb and forefinger and waved it at me in broad daylight. Hypnotized, I reached the lobby door, all thoughts of Roy completely gone.

I reached for the doorknob and turned it, the latch clicking back. Pulling on the heavy glass door, it swung open with a final squeal of warning. But I did not take it's heed. Instead, I stepped aside and in two steps, the big, black man was inside my building.

He flipped the massive erection back into his shorts as he stepped past me, stopped and waited for me. I turned and led the way to the elevator.

He stood beside me, quietly, as I punched the call button. The elevator came and the door opened. Old Mrs. Mancuso from 6-F, down the hall from me, toddled out. She greeted me as she shuffled past and stared disapprovingly at the stranger.

"You live alone?" The black man asked when Mrs. Mancuso was out of earshot. I shook my head, surprised that I had lied so easily.

The black man grunted. "What about the roof?"

"It's locked." My voice sounded small and distant to me. I had visions of being beat up, then thrown off the roof after I had given myself to him.

The big, black man looked at me. I could feel him glaring behind the mirrored sunglasses. I looked up and saw my reflection, small and meek.

"Well, fuck this shit, man!" He drawled and pushed me into the elevator. "I'm gonna get me some white boy pussy if I have to fuck you in broad daylight!"

The elevator door closed and without thinking, I punched the button with the gold letter "B." The elevator slowly moved down as the big, black man pushed himself against me, his face inches from mine. His hard cock rubbed against my bulging crotch and I sighed as he reached down and squeezed it roughly. He grinned, his teeth blinding white. I looked up at him, trying to see through the sunglasses but all I got was my own reflection; brown eyes staring back with excitement and fear, cock-hungry lips quivering with anticipation.

"You like black dick, boy?" He teased, grinding his hips against me.

"I . . . I dunno. I guess."

"You guess?" The elevator stopped. "Where in the basement we goin'?"

"The laundry room?" I suggested. The door opened and the hallway yawned before us. He pushed me out.

The laundry room was empty. I stepped in and he followed. He poked his head out into the hallway, looked both ways, then shut the door behind him and locked it. The audible click reverberated in my head, loud and ominous. For just a moment, I shivered.

*What the hell am I doing? Why am I so scared?*

Then he faced me. My eyes automatically dropped down to his still hard cock and I swallowed hard, confronting my irrational fear.

"What exactly do you want from me?" I tried to make conversation.

"Boy, if you have to ask, you're dumber than shit!" He laughed and walked slowly towards me.

I stepped back, knowing full well what it was he wanted. My heart beat loudly in my head as he approached me.

He put his hands on my shoulders and I felt my body stiffen. But then the warmth emanating from his hands spread through my shoulders and down my neck, back and chest. I felt a relaxation flow into my belly and down the rest of my body until it reached my toes. I knew what I wanted and, suddenly, I no longer felt scared.

"Sit down!" I felt him nudging me toward a bench to my right.

As I sat, he pushed his red shorts down, letting them drop down to his feet. He kicked them aside and with his left hand grabbed his hard black prick by the root.

"Okay, boy. Start sucking!" He waved it at me, the head of his chocolate brown fuck stick less than an inch away from my lips.

"There's something you should know." I looked up at him. He blinked down at me, a look of annoyance flashing across his face.

"Whatever it is, I don't give a shit, boy! Now start sucking! Or am I gonna have to force feed you?"

His dick jumped, and, taking the plunge, I opened my mouth. I stuck my tongue out, licking at the pinkish-brown cockhead. He sighed. Encouraged, I grabbed his engorged meat by the base and licked the shaft until it was slippery and wet from my spit. I ran my fist over it, stroking him as I cupped his balls. They were heavy and moist and hot.

"That's it, boy. Suck on my nuts!" He pushed at the back of my head and forced me to come closer. Instinctively, my mouth opened and I sucked the big, brown balls of flesh into my mouth; first one, then the other. I took a deep breath and the intoxicating aroma of his sweat rushed through my head.

"Now the dick, boy! Work the dick!"

But I needed no further prompting. Virgin or not, I took to sucking cock like a duck to water. I popped his balls out of my mouth and sucked on the head of his juicy fuckpole, shoving the tip of my tongue into his piss slit. Pre-cum drooled out and I slurped on it greedily.

He placed a hand at the back of my neck, forcing me to take more of his hard black meat. But he was so huge, and I so inexperienced, that all I could handle was about four inches of dick before gagging and choking.

I worked on his heavy balls with my left hand, stroking the length of dick I couldn't accommodate down my throat with my right. My lips slid across the long fuckstick as I bobbed my head back and forth. He groaned. Grabbing me by the ears, he began to pump faster. Thinking he was about to come, I sped up; but he pulled out, grabbed his dick by the base and slapped me across the face with it.

"Not yet, mother fucker! What's your rush?!"

"But I thought you . . ."

"I'm not cumming yet," he chuckled. "There's something else I want."

He lifted me up by the armpits, as if I were a baby, and he sat me down on the padded table beside the bench. He pulled off my tee-shirt and pushed me back against the table, lengthwise. I could feel the cracked vinyl against my skin. Then he tugged at my shorts and underwear, his hands rough on my flesh. He whistled admiringly as my cock slapped my belly.

"Nice dick for a white boy. What you might call . . . party size." He wrapped his fist around my dick and stroked it a couple of times. Then he climbed on the table with his ass to me and lowered it down onto my face. Spreading his beefy black buns apart, the puckered hole winked at me.

"C'mon, boy! Stick your tongue up my black hole! Dontcha know how to eat ass?!" I hesitated. "C'mon, now! Stick your tongue out and clean out my asshole!"

He groaned as I licked it and started to tongue fuck him, slicking up his asshole. He rubbed his ass over my face and mouth, then leaned forward and sucked the entire length of my cock into his practiced mouth. The head slid down past his expert throat as he worked the shaft with his fist.

My cock throbbed, dangerously close to shooting a load. He sensed it and pulled back, sighing as he pushed his ass further onto my face. My tongue was buried deeper in his rectum, my face full of his sweat and my spit, thoughts of Roy all but forgotten.

After a moment, the black man got off the table and walked around to the edge where my feet were dangling. He pulled me towards him, grabbed me by the ankles and threw my legs up in the air so my ass was exposed.

My virgin butthole twitched in anticipation and I held my breath, wondering what he was about to do. Then I felt his long, pink tongue tease the puckered entrance. I moaned and writhed on the table as he darted it in and out of my sweaty asshole. While he ate my ass, he worked a thick, long finger inside me. Then, when it was in, he finger fucked me while I held my own legs up for him.

"You're not gonna fuck me are you?"

"What do you think?" A shit-eating grin flashed across his face.

"Please, there's something you should know."

"What's that?"

"I'm still a virgin."

The big, black man laughed. "Yeah, right! And I'm the fucking Easter Bunny."

"No, really! I am! I tried to tell you befo . . . *ohhhhhhhh!!!*"

The man's finger hit my prostate and I closed my eyes, relishing the sensation.

"Hmmm. You see? I knew you were lying. Man, you are gonna love getting fucked by this big, black cock!"

I chose not to argue the point. "Oh, who cares! Fuck me, please!" I begged him, whispering. I sighed as he rubbed my prostate even more, working a second finger up my shithole.

"You really want my black dick up your little white ass?" His grin grew wider. I nodded and heard myself whimper as he rotated his fingers around inside me, spreading the lips open. "You like black meat?" I nodded shamelessly, overtaken by the sensations coursing through my body. I would have agreed to anything so I long as I got him to fuck me.

"C'mon, man! Just fuck me already! Quit messing around and shove that big black thing up my ass!"

He pulled his fingers out of my ass and I cried out. It felt as if my hole had been ripped; but I still wanted him to fuck me. I wanted him to take me and possess me fully; to pound me until I saw heaven.

I let my legs go and stretched them out a moment before he bent them at the knees and braced the bottoms of my feet on top of the table.

Grabbing his stiff prick by the base with his left hand, the big, black man raised his right hand up to his mouth and spit into the palm. He slicked the head of his cock and positioned himself, pressing the head up against my hole.

"Please be careful. I really am a virgin, you know!"

"Bull-fucking-shit!" He replied and pushed forcefully. The fat knob of his cockhead split my asshole and popped in painfully. I opened my mouth to scream, but bit my tongue instead. I didn't want anyone hearing me, bursting into the laundry room and finding me this way, a huge black cock up my ass. I was aware of my dick going limp and tears streaming from the corners of my eyes and into my ears.

He pushed again, not bothering to give me time to grow accustomed to the sensation of his cock invading me. I felt as a few more inches ripped deeper into my fuckhole. A stabbing pain pierced through me as I focused my energy on my violated asshole, forcing it to relax. But my sphincter only tightened up, clamping down on the thick shaft impaling me. I threw my arms over my face, covering my eyes so that he wouldn't see me cry.

The big, black man pushed on.

Time stood still and I thought I might have passed out. Then I felt his pubic hair scratch at my ass and the pain, miraculously enough, started to ebb. He leaned forward and licked at my throat, slowly grinding his hips from side to side. I wrapped my legs around his waist and felt my nipples harden as he bit into my neck.

"Oh, man! I can't believe this!" I murmured.

"What's that, sugar lips?" Buried deep inside me, his demeanor suddenly changed. He seemed capable of tenderness.

"Your cock! My hole!" My breath was still short. "I just can't believe it's all inside me." I felt him touch something within me that was more than just about getting fucked.

"Let me know when your ready." He raised himself up a little and looked into my eyes, a smile playing on his lips. "You really a virgin?" I nodded as his fingers probed at the raw, stretched opening that was my fuckhole. He raised his fingers up to the light. They came away with a couple of droplets of blood. We both looked at them. Then he brought his fingers down to my lips. I opened my mouth and sucked deeply on them. I moaned when he pulled the fingers out.

"I'm ready."

He kissed me. Then, slowly, he threw my legs over his shoulders and gently slid his hard dick from my hole. Just as gently, he slid it back in. Taking my left hand in his right, he then made me reach down to where his dick spread my chute. I wrapped my fingers around the base of his prick as he thrust balls deep into me and my cock stiffened. He reached up to my chest and tweaked my nipples. Bending over, he bit and chewed on them, pulling with sharp white teeth. His cockhead massaged my prostate as he fucked me.

Standing up, he thrust harder, pounding my ass. His hips became a dark blur as his balls swayed to and fro, his cock slamming in and out of me like a battering ram. He grabbed my hard dick in his big black hand and stroked it hot and fast. My balls jumped up and down and I felt the table underneath me rocking dangerously. Our skin smacked loudly as he slammed into me again and again.

"Oh, baby! I can't hold it much longer. You want it, boy? You want my load? You want to feel me cumming inside you?"

"Yes! Oh, *yes!*" I sighed, tweaking my own nipples.

The big, black man pulled his cock out almost all the way and plunged it all back in one final time. The entire length of his thick, hard tool sank deep into my bowels. He groaned and threw his head back as his throbbing shaft shot his load up my twitching asshole.

He fisted my dick, pushing down hard, as if trying to pull the foreskin off. I shot a wild load. The first spurt thwacked at the wall just above my head. The rest spurt into the air and landed on my belly in a thick puddle.

We stayed that way until our breathing returned to normal, our bodies glued together by our sweat and my cum.

After a moment, sweat running down his face and neck, the black man stood. His tee-shirt clung to him as he put his hand to my face and held out his fingers. I sucked on each of them, one by one, licking my own cum off his flesh. While I sucked on his last finger, he pulled the thick slab of meat out of my ass slowly. I felt every inch of the fat dick he'd managed to cram up in my bowels. It felt as if I were taking a long, painful shit. It came away with a loud slurp and I gasped at the sudden emptiness deep within me.

He walked around the table, his limp cock dangling near my mouth. I closed my eyes and sucked on the cum smeared meat, tasting his salty load mixed with my ass juices; the sweat and blood of my own asshole.

When his dick was clean, he pulled his cock from my mouth. I whimpered. He picked up his shorts, stepped into them and stuffed the hardening prick back into them. It was a shame to watch it disappear.

"Will I see you again?" I blurted.

"Sorry, sugar lips. This black man doesn't fuck the same ass twice."

"But . . ." I started to protest. He turned and walked out of the laundry room, leaving the door wide open. I got up and dressed as quickly as I could, but by the time I got to the elevator, he was gone. Dejected, I rode the elevator back up to my apartment.

As I made my way the hallway, I could hear my phone ringing.

"Hello?" I answered once inside. I felt something hot and thick ooze out of my hole. I reached into my pants and dabbed at my hole. My fingertips came away with some of the black man's sperm on them. I put the fingers in my mouth and sucked on the tips as more of the load trickled down my inner thighs.

"Hey, little buddy. It's me."

"Roy! Where have you been? I waited almost an hour for you! I thought you stood me up!"

"And miss that virgin ass of yours? No way! I'm sorry, but I was stuck on a train. I've been at the station over half an hour now. Where have you been? I tried calling." He sounded as if he were accusing me.

*Getting fucked!* I thought to myself and giggled quietly.

"I was . . . doing laundry." I replied with a smile.

"Can I come up?" Roy asked. He sounded eager. I felt my butthole twitch with anticipation and more sperm flowed out.

"What the hell. I've got some catching up to do."

"What do you mean?"

"Oh, nothing. I'll explain when I see. Why don't you just come on up here? It's real easy." I gave Roy directions, the code to let himself in, and went to wait for him on my bed with my freshly fucked ass up in the air.

# A Walk In The Park

The heat of a summer day is like a lover's touch or a sensual kiss that lingers against the flesh of your throat. It's like the feel of a man's tongue as he licks his way from your nipples down to your belly and, finally, down to your cock and balls.

On such a day I called in sick. I couldn't bear the thought of being inside a stuffy office building. Then, after a shower and some breakfast, I left my apartment and went for a walk in the park. Since it was a workday, I knew it wouldn't be crowded. I figured I'd find a quiet, secluded spot where I could take my tee-shirt off, kick back, and relax in the sun.

While taking my walk, however, I got the sudden urge to take a leak. Too much coffee will sometimes do that to me. Making sure there was no one around, I stood in front of a large tree and pulled the front of my shorts down. I whipped my dick out, and just as I began to let go, I heard leaves crunch and twigs snap. I quickly pulled my shorts back up, my cock about to burst.

What I saw made me moan and my bladder almost let go. He was a short, dark-skinned latin man with thick black hair, bushy eyebrows and a mustache. His eyes were black as coal, his lips full, red and sensuous.

He looked up at me as he broke through the trees, walking with a 10-speed bicycle by his side.

I devoured him visually, admiring the shirtless, wiry body. His skin was smooth, his chest well defined, with dark brown areolas the size of half-dollars. The nipples were large and erect, his belly flat and smooth. Just the slightest hint of black hair around his belly button led down to the goods. His hips were wide underneath a pair of black, Spandex bicycle shorts and his thighs were thick and muscular, the legs hairy.

I sucked in a deep breath when I saw the outline of his cock, clearly visible against his right thigh, underneath the tight, stretched material. I could even make out the ridge of his cockhead and knew he was cut. To the untrained eye, it might have appeared hard, but I knew better. It was about five inches long, soft. I could just imagine the lengths it was capable of and drooled at the thought.

He glanced at me once more as he walked by and our eyes met. He did not smile, nod, or acknowledge my admiration for him; but he looked over his right shoulder as he walked past and I knew he could be had. I had yet to come across a latin man that could refuse the beguiling ways and talents of a blonde boy's expert mouth, or his smooth, tight ass.

The urge to piss began to subside, replaced now, by the desire to see up close what the man had between his legs; to thrust my tongue up his musk-scented asshole and bury my face in his crack.

The sight of his juicy, round globes moving up and down within the confines of the skin-tight pants only served to urge me forward. I started walking after him, wondering what he would do when he realized he was being followed. There was always the possibility he might not be interested, but that was part of the excitement.

I tailed him as he walked his bike down the hill and onto a path. The short latin man looked over his shoulder, finally aware he was being followed. He did nothing to deter me, nor did he increase his gait. Once on the bike path, however, he jumped onto his bicycle and slowly pedaled away. He glanced over his shoulder a final time, grinned at me and sped away.

"Shit!" I muttered, feeling foolish.

The nerve of that cockteaser! Now I was practically hard and it showed through my shorts. And to make matters worse, the urge to piss had returned. I decided to skip watering the trees and see what was happening at the public men's room, just down the bike path, near the playground.

Inside, the small rest room was empty and smelled of stale piss. There were three urinals along the right wall, on the opposite wall were four stalls with no doors. You couldn't even sit down in private, but at least they had toilet paper. I was glad I only had to take a leak.

Stepping up to the last urinal, I managed to piss after my hard-on went down. When I was finished, I shook my cock vigorously and felt the veins beginning to fill again.

*Damn that short latin man!*

He had gotten me all hot and bothered and now all I could think about was sitting in one of the stalls to wait and see what showed up. Suck the first thing that came along. But I didn't do it. Instead, I tucked my cock back inside my shorts and left.

Outside, parents sat watching their children play, old people sat on benches silently reading or playing chess.

I walked past the monkey bars, see-saws and kiddy swings where children squealed with delight. I headed straight for the big-kid swings which were several yards away, facing the men's room. I figured if I was going to go after any public men's room meat, I would sit and watch from there rather than inside.

I sat on one of the swings and started gaining some momentum. From there, too, I could see the water fountain just outside the door to the men's room. I watched every single guy that strode up to the water fountain just before going inside to take a piss; then stop and take another drink on their way out, filling their bladders up again. Several of them were actually worth stopping the swing for, to go and check out, but I didn't. I was enjoying the breeze too much.

After a short time, the latin bicyclist suddenly stepped up to the water fountain and bent over for a drink.

I watched, enraptured, as he cupped water in his hands and splashed it over his face, neck and chest. I

70

imagined the taste of his sweat on my tongue as I licked the sides of his neck, bit his throat and worked my way down to his navel. Then, while I let the swing start to slow down, he stood up, turned, and looked right at me. He wasn't so far away that I couldn't see the recognition in his eyes. He didn't smile or wave. Instead, he stepped away from the water fountain, propped his bicycle up on the kickstand, and facing me, started to stretch. He looked as if he were cooling down, but I knew he was putting on a private show for me.

He raised his muscled arms up in the air, exposing his sweaty, hairy armpits. I nearly swooned, imagining that I was burying my face in them and inhaling deeply.

Every once in a while he would turn and look to make sure I was still watching him. I could see the length of meat in his pants growing longer and thicker. Then, making sure I was watching, he pulled the front of his pants away from his belly, reached inside with his right hand and rearranged his growing cock so that it lay flat against his groin. I couldn't help licking my lips and he finally smiled, showing straight, white teeth. He knew I was hooked and it was quite obvious by now he was enjoying teasing me. Latin men love knowing a cocksucker is getting off watching them.

The latin man turned all of a sudden and went to his bike. He walked it into the men's room and I jumped off the still moving swing, my cock stiff and aching, tenting the front of my shorts.

At the doorway to the men's room, he turned and looked over his shoulder. He stood there a moment, our eyes locked. Then he walked inside. I followed with my hands in front of me, trying to cover my erection and look cool. But no one noticed anything and I slipped inside.

After being in the sun for so long, the darkness blinded me a moment. When my eyes adjusted, I saw a pair of feet in the last stall facing the toilet. I could hear him pissing, a sound that echoed inside the public rest room. His bicycle leaned against the far wall, near the stall. There was no one else there.

I stepped up to the last urinal and turned my head to look at him. Standing with his back to me, he turned his head when he heard me coming and continued to piss. It sounded as if he had been holding the amber liquid back for some time. I pretended to piss, the beat of my heart pounding in my head. When I realized that he had stopped, I glanced over my shoulder again and saw that he had turned completely around to face me. I looked down and my mouth dropped open at the sight of his cock.

He had lowered the waistband of his Spandex to underneath his bulging balls. He stood with his left hand on his hip while his right slowly stroked the length of his stiff prick. How such a short guy could have been endowed with such a huge cock was beyond me. He was shorter than me and I was only five feet six! But his cock more than made up for his lack of stature. It was a tremendously juicy slab of meat about ten inches long and about six inches fat around. The mushroom head was large and pink, swollen to the size of a baby's fist. As I watched, he stroked and squeezed his cock. As his hand went up toward the head, a drop of pre-cum oozed out of the wide piss slit. Hungry, I took a step toward him.

"No!" He whispered. "In there!" He nodded toward the stall beside his. I hurried into the stall, pulling my shorts down as I sat on the toilet.

Facing the partition, the latin man sank to his knees and pushed his thighs underneath. His hard cock was aimed up at me, bobbing for attention. The top of it pressed against the underside of the partition and it looked even more swollen; as if he'd been wearing a cockring. I spit into the palms of my hands, wrapped the right around the base of my own stiff prick, then reached out with my left and wrapped my fingers around the base of the latin monument begging me to pay homage to it.

I stroked it lovingly, pumping it expertly, running my fist along the entire length. He was silent and for a brief moment, I was worried. Could I truly satisfy this latin stud kneeling on the dirty floor in the stall beside me? But I banished all doubt from my mind and decided that I didn't really care if he was satisfied or not. My prime concern was with tasting that cock and taking as much of it down my throat as I could. My own satisfaction was what I had in mind, and if he was satisfied in the process, that was merely icing on the cake.

I bent over, opened my mouth, and wrapped my lips around the thick, swollen head of his cock. He moaned softly.

I placed the tip of my tongue in his piss slit, tasting pre-cum. Unable to reach his cock completely, I released it and got down on my hands and knees on the dirty floor. I cupped his big balls in one hand and licked at the sides of his swollen cock. Then, hungry for his huge piece of meat, I opened my mouth wide. I allowed the big, thick tool to stretch my jaw and nearly swallowed it whole. Gagging, I pulled back and bobbed my head up and down, my lips stroking the shaft further and further with each downward stroke, stretching for the base.

After a few minutes, however, I suddenly released it. I was growing nervous about the lack of doors on the stalls, and although I hadn't heard anyone come in, I wasn't pleased with the thought of someone catching me with a dick down my throat; at least, not in a public men's room. I sat back down on the toilet and looked down at the latin man's thighs, his throbbing, massive erection.

"Wanna go someplace else?" I grabbed a hold of his shaft and pumped.

"This is a fuckin' park, man! Where we gonna go?!" His English was slightly accented. I imagined him whispering dirty Spanish things into my ear as he slowly fucked me.

"We can go back to the hill. Where I first saw you. It seemed pretty quiet there," I replied. He stayed where he was for a moment, apparently weighing the suggestion. Then he pulled away, his thick cock sliding out of my hand. I heard him pull his Spandex up and he went for his bike.

"Wait a few minutes before following me out." He walked past me with his bike, and stepped outside.

I waited a moment or two, flushed the toilet, then stood and pulled my pants up before heading back to the area where we first encountered one another.

The latin man had propped his bicycle up against a huge tree several feet away from the main path, secluding us for privacy. Then he turned and stood with his legs spread wide, hands on hips; a tempting, teasing pose that made my mouth water and my cock tingle.

As I approached, he slipped his thumbs into the waistband of the Spandex and pulled them down. He turned around slowly and bent over, thrusting his beefy buns out at me. My tongue wagged at the sight of his hairy cheeks and I sprinted the last few feet toward him. I barely felt the twigs scrape against my flesh as I dropped to my knees to worship his asshole.

The latin man reached behind him and pulled his own buns apart. I looked at the glistening, puckered hole a moment, all covered with hair, before diving in. Parting back the coarse hair that covered the sweaty entrance, I was delighted to find it was a darker brown than the rest of him, as were his dick and balls. I closed my eyes and buried my face in his hairy crack, my nose right in his bunghole. I inhaled deeply, me head reeling from the musky, sweaty scent of his asshole. I planted a kiss on the puckered entrance, stuck my tongue out, then licked it.

"Yeah! Lick my Puerto Rican hole, baby! Eat me out and clean it up!" He commanded, but I needed no prodding.

As I thrust my tongue in and out of his sweaty hole, he reached behind and grabbed the back of my head, forcing me deeper into his bottom. He suddenly went wild, rubbing his ass up and down against my face, pushing back against me. For a moment, I thought I would suffocate. But I didn't care. If I died with my tongue up such a delicious tasting asshole I would be happy.

My cock, stiff between my legs, was still inside my shorts. I'd been unable to release it and I could feel myself drooling pre-cum. Latin men always excited me that way.

After a while, the latin man pulled his ass away from my tongue and stood up. He turned around and slapped me in the face with his thick, hard, brown slab of meat. It was like getting hit with a small bat. I opened my mouth, trying to grab a hold of it with my lips, but he kept swinging his hips from left to right, his hands on my head, whacking me with his stiff cock. It was hard as a rock and hurt my face as he whipped it back and forth, but I didn't want him to stop.

All of a sudden, he stood perfectly still, aimed the thick, swollen head at my mouth and shoved it inside. I gagged as the tip brushed past my throat, tears welling in my eyes. I reached down between my legs and pulled my cock out. Wrapping my hand around the base, I started pumping. I wanted to come, but I wouldn't. Not until he shot a healthy, tangy load and I felt it sliding down past my throat.

He placed his hands on either side of my head and thrust his cock in and out of my mouth, fucking my face with wild abandon. His big ball sac banged hard against my chin and I wondered why he didn't cry out in pain. A few times, the entire length of his shaft slid down my throat and his pubic hair brushed against my nose. I wanted the latin skullfucker to bury his cock balls-deep in my mouth and shoot his load that way, but my jaw was beginning to ache and my throat felt raw. I felt him start speed up, his thrusts becoming relentless. A low growl began to build deep within him.

"Don't swallow it!" He warned between clenched teeth. "Keep it in your mouth so you can feed it to me!" And a split second later, he let loose with a loud grunt. His pulsating cock spewed in my mouth and the first volley hit the back of my throat with brutal force. Instinctively, I swallowed that first spurt, then remembered what he wanted me to do.

His hot seed filled my mouth, my cheeks puffing out as his load bathed the head of his cock. He came so copiously that my mouth was full before he was even finished. Some of it was fucked out of my mouth by his still pumping hips and it oozed out the sides, dripping down my jaw.

Finally, he stopped, his breathing still hard and fast. Looking down at me, he suddenly laughed. I could just imagine what I looked like kneeling there before him; my aching cock in hand, balls swaying back and forth as I continued stroking. I would have laughed myself, except I would have spilled his seed.

He motioned for me to stand up, then leaned forward and his mouth met mine. Grabbing my face in his left hand, he squeezed my cheeks roughly while kissing me. His hot load flowed from my mouth and into his. Then he abruptly pulled away and dropped to his knees. I thought he was going to suck me off, but instead, he grabbed me by the hips and spun me around, yanking at my shorts.

The calluses of his small, rough hands against my smooth ass made my flesh tingle as he spread my buns apart. My asshole twitched with anticipation. I knew he was going to eat me and that I was about to get fucked.

And he was using his own cum as lube!

The very thought sent shivers of pleasure down my spine. I felt my asshole relax, pucker tight, then open again, as if it were breathing. I heard him moan just before he shoved his tongue into me. I took a deep breath and sighed.

His puckered lips met mine, anxiously awaiting the flow of cum from his mouth and the probing tongue. I felt the still hot cream slowly oozed out of his mouth and into my fuckhole. He used his tongue to get it all in, bathing the sides of my rectum with spit and sperm, lapping at nearly spilled drops.

"You ever get fucked by a dirty Rican before?"

"No, never!" I lied with a shake of my head. Why bother spoiling his fun?

He pushed me roughly against the nearby tree, my face pressing into the bark. I opened my arms and wrapped them around the trunk as if I were hugged a huge teddy bear. The latin man stood up and I felt him behind me, teasing my opening with the tip of his cock. I moaned loudly.

"Please!" I begged him. "Fuck me! Shove that big latin cock up my ass!"

"You really want it?" He pressed against me. The tip almost, but not quite, penetrated my spasming hole.

"Yes! I really want it!" I moaned, practically in tears.

"What do you want me to do with it?" He pushed again, ever so slightly. The head of his hard, Puerto Rican meat plunged into me and stayed there without moving. I gasped from the sudden intrusion but didn't move away.

"I want you to fuck me with it! I want to feel that bad boy ramming me, hard and fast, pumping me full of your hard, latin meat. I want you to stuff me with that dirty thing until I scream!"

I felt him push suddenly. The tender sides of my asshole yielded and the thick, swollen glans that was his cockhead plunged deeper within me. I moaned with pain, and he with pleasure. I glanced around to make sure no one was coming near. He was oblivious.

Latin men were all the same when it came to fucking. The only things that existed for them were their cocks and the tight assholes they were penetrating.

I watched the short latin man look down at his cock as he split my cheeks apart and impaled me. He pushed further and deeper, spearing me with his thick pole. His lips pursed together and his eyes narrowed at the sight of his meat disappearing inside me. I knew the sight well; I got off on it whenever I got the chance to fuck. It was a sight that drove men wild. The bigger the cock, the tighter the hole felt. The tighter the hole felt, the wilder the desire to ram in all the way in to the balls.

I tried to relax as the latin fucker thrust more of his cock into me. I had already taken almost half of it and I was full. I glanced over my shoulder again and caught him as he opened his mouth and spit. I felt it land at the tender junction of my raw hole and his turgid pole. Then, grabbing me by the waist, he pulled my hips closer to him, impaling me with his thick, long spear. I cried out, pleasure now mixing with the pain.

I felt as every inch slowly disappeared inside me. Then he stopped and groaned as the final inch slid home. His coarse pubic bush scraped against my backside. His groin was pressed so tight against me that I couldn't wedge my hand between us.

"Oh man!" The little latin man moaned. "I can't believe you took the whole thing!"

In response, I reached between my legs and squeezed his balls. "Shut up and slam that Puerto Rican cock in and out of my white ass!"

"With pleasure!" He pulled out slowly, his meat tugging at the insides of my rectum and turning me inside out. It seemed incredibly long and I felt as if I were taking a long, hard shit. Then he stopped, with only the pulsating head of his cock inside me. Then, ever so slowly, he inched it all back in with one steady forward stroke, like a hot knife through butter. I moaned with delirious pleasure as the tip rubbed against my prostate. I knew it would not be long before I shot my load all over the tree.

After sinking the entire length of his shaft back inside me, the latin man leaned his weight against me, pushing my hips back into the tree. I held on for dear life, my face pressed into the bard. Rough edges scraped my nipples and I moaned even more, my stiff cock flat against my belly.

As the latin man pulled out and rammed his cock back inside me, my cock rubbed against the tree trunk. It was somewhat uncomfortable, but between the pleasure of getting my hole vigorously plowed and the pain of rubbing my smooth flesh and cock against the tree, I felt myself getting close.

"C'mon, fucker! Do me, man! Give it to me!" I cried.

The short latin man with the big dick started to slam in and out of me, ripping and stretching my raw and abused manhole, touching me to the very core of my being. My cock throbbed and my balls tingled as I got ready to shoot my load.

"I'm gonna cum!" I cried.

He thrust his cock forward and buried it balls deep inside me, corkscrewing into me while reaching around to twist my already agonized nipples. I moaned out loud then, and came with a cry that disturbed the birds in the trees. Thick, creamy spunk shot out of my cock and bathed the tree trunk. I was still pressed up against it and felt as my load smeared against my belly, my asshole twitching around the thick tube of meat pumping inside me.

Seconds later, I felt him trembling behind me, his cock pulsating, and I knew he was ready. He pulled his cock out entirely, then roughly slammed it back in one final time, knocking the wind out of me. He bit down at the base of my neck and groaned as he shot a steamy load inside me. He kept grinding, pushing me further into the tree. A jagged piece of bark dug into my left nipple and I bit back a cry of pain.

We remained that way until he'd caught his breath. Then he pulled out. His meat slurped noisily and slapped against his thigh with a wet, smacking sound. I turned to look at it and it was all I could do to drop to my knees and clean it up. It was all covered with sweat, spit, sperm and asshole juices.

I fell to the ground, however, my knees suddenly weak. But I was happy and satisfied as I lay on my back, waiting for my breath to come back to normal. We looked at each other and smiled.

"You're bleeding." He pointed at my nipple. It was the piece of bark that dug into me when he came up my ass. He clamped his mouth over my nipple and started to suck. It hurt and I pushed him away.

"Whassa matter? Can't take a little pain?" He smiled cockily at me.

"Only when I'm being fucked." I looked between his legs and saw his cock start to twitch.

"So what are you saying? Wanna get dicked again?"

"I don't know. I'm not so sure." I reached between my legs and felt my bunghole. His cum was starting to ooze out.

"What? Didn't I get you worked up enough?" He snickered. We looked into each other's eyes and I could feel the desire in my body welling up again. My cock twitched and I knew I would be ready for another round soon. He looked at my cock and smiled. "So? Wanna go for round two?"

"Yeah," I said finally, smiling back at me. "But let's go back to my place. This time I wanna ride you like you ride that bicycle."

The short latin man stood up and looked down at me. I smiled back.

"Is that right?" He said, a cocky, shit eating grin on his face.

"Yeah! I'm gonna sit on your face and pedal your ears!" I replied and we both laughed.

"Well, then, what the hell are we waiting for? Let's go!" He helped me up, mounted his bicycle and pedaled slowly beside me.

I couldn't wait to get home!

# Subway Pick-Up

"Well, gentlemen! It's been a lovely evening but I'm afraid I must be getting home."

"Are you sure? You're welcome to stay, you know." Tony, my ex-lover of four years, tried to persuade me.

"Thank you, but, it's pretty late."

"Oh c'mon! It's not *that* late!" Tony's new lover, Tom, piped in. His voice slurred. Tony had been plying him full of drinks from the start of the evening.

"It's 2:00 a.m., Tom. I have a lot of things to do tomorrow." I stood from the couch and stretched. Tony wasn't far behind; he'd been eyeing me the entire evening. I'd seen that look many times during the four years we were together. I knew what he wanted, but he wasn't going to get it from me. As soon as I left, Tony would pounce on poor Tom and probably wouldn't let up until dawn.

"You know, we really don't mind if you spend the night, would we hon?" Tom wrapped an arm around Tony's waist and looked up at him the way I used to; with passion and desire. But that was another time and another life.

Tony shook his head in response. "He's right. We don't mind. Sure you won't stay? It gets pretty creepy on the subway late at night. At least take a cab."

I smiled, looking deep into Tony's dark eyes. I glanced down and saw the rapidly growing mound of flesh I used to spend so many hours making love to. Something inside me burned feverishly and I knew that if I stayed we would wind up in a three-way. It wasn't the three-way I minded; just sharing Tony with Tom.

"Thank you, but I'll be fine. And thanks, Tom, for a wonderful dinner. I had a great time."

I turned and headed for the door. Tony was behind me, alarmingly close. I could feel the sexual heat from his thick, hairy body rolling off him in waves.

"Call me when you get home." I turned to look at him. He shrugged. "I just wanna make sure you got in okay."

"Thanks for the concern, Tony. But just because this is Brooklyn doesn't mean it's uncivilized. I'll call you next week. Good night, guys."

"Be careful!" They called in unison as I walked down the corridor towards the elevator. I punched the call button and waved to them as I stepped inside.

I yawned as the elevator started to move. I looked at my watch. It was 2:10 already. I hoped the train came quick!

Inside their air conditioned apartment, I'd forgotten about the oppressive heat outside. It was unusually hot for early summer. As I walked through the lobby and onto the sidewalk, a light coating of sweat covered my smooth, hairless body. Between the heat and the memory of sex with Tony, I was beside myself with perverse thoughts. I didn't just want to get off, though. I wanted to be taken, used and abused. I wanted to be left spent and wasted with nothing left to give except my cock for whoever wanted to use it as a piece of meat. I was beyond horny; I was in fucking heat!

The Newkirk Avenue station, on the D line, was only a few blocks away. The entrance and turnstiles were street level, but the tracks were underground and open to the sky. The people that lived in the small walk-ups surrounding the plaza could look out their windows and see the passing of the trains. It made for a more appealing ride but the delays were horrendous when it rained or snowed.

I walked up to the clerk in the booth and slipped a twenty through the slot.

"One, please." The Metropolitan Transit Authority had switched to swipe cards a couple of years ago, but I still liked the feel of tokens.

The clerk counted out my change, then shoved it through the slot with the token on top. I stuffed the change into a back pocket and clutched the token in my right hand. I turned towards the turnstiles and that was when I spotted the Puerto Rican boy standing near the booth. Dressed in a billowing, white tee-shirt and black, baggy jeans, he looked to be about nineteen. His face was dark and sexually alive.

I drank in the sight of his slender build. My knees weakened and my asshole twitched at the sight of the bulge between his legs; even through his baggy clothes.

I plunged the token through the slot and went through the heavy, wooden turnstile. On the other side, I turned and looked over my right shoulder. The boy was watching me. He hooked his right thumb into the right front pocket, his other fingers curling around, and framing, his mouth-watering bulge. I thought he squeezed an invitation, but I was too far away to be sure.

A little voice inside my head went off and instantly put me on guard. I had heard stories of butch boys who cruised gay guys for sex, then beat them up for their money. Had he seen how much money I had on me? I only had a little under twenty dollars, but people have been mugged for a lot less. Perhaps I should have taken a cab after all.

I shot a cautious glance back over my shoulder, saw him look away, then ran down the few steps before he had a chance to see what direction I was taking.

At the bottom of those steps was a landing. The stairs on the left led to trains going Downtown and into Manhattan. The stairs on the right led to trains going to Sheepshead Bay, Brighton Beach and Coney Island.

On the landing, standing between the two directional signs, was a transit cop. The man in uniform had thick, dark blond hair that peeked out from underneath his cap. A mustache, trim and well kept, crowned a full, red upper lip. Hard, dark brown eyes caught mine as I went down the steps. I couldn't help noticing the way he stood. His legs were spread slightly apart and he held his nightstick in front of him with both hands, resting on an appetizing mound. I wondered if his cock was as thick as his billyclub. A tingling warmed my balls as I envisioned the tough-looking Rican boy whipping out his cock and the cop using his nightstick to lift it up, instead of using his hand.

The cop nodded at me, then straight head. As I turned right and went down the stairs, I could feel his eyes on me.

That late at night, the train would be short. I walked to the front of the platform, sat down in the middle of the brown wooden bench and stretched my legs out before me, spreading them. I rested my arms along the length of the bench and threw my head back. Sweat trickled down my back and I could feel it on my scalp. The light breeze wasn't enough to cool my sweaty, low-hanging balls, but it did make my dick stir.

My thoughts turned to the Puerto Rican with the big, round bulge, then the hot cop with the big, fat nightstick. I reached between my legs, stuck a couple of fingers up my shorts and scratched my balls. They came away wet and musky. I put them in my mouth and sucked. Almost immediately, my dick began to harden. I shifted my legs and licked my lips. The salty taste of sweat aroused me even more.

*Damn! Where the hell IS that train?!*

I wanted to get home quick so I could jerk off, fantasizing about the Puerto Rican and the cop with his nightstick.

I wondered if the boy's basket was stuffed with balls or cockmeat. I was thinking I would have liked to find out, when out of the corner of my eyes, I saw someone coming down the steps. I turned to look. It was the Puerto Rican boy.

He moved slowly and deliberately, hands in his front pockets. A stony glare was etched on his face. I noticed that he was a bit on the grungy side; a scrub 'n fuck. No matter how many times you scrubbed him, he'd still be dirty; but it worked for him.

His black hair was cropped close to the scalp and his skin was a deep shade of tan. Long eyelashes surrounded brown, puppy dog eyes and he sported a fine, almost non-existent mustache. His lower lip protruded in a petulant pout and I imagined myself biting it as I kissed him. My dick stiffened even more as I envisioned them wrapped around my pulsating shaft.

The boy walked towards me, aware that he was being watched. My heartbeat quickened and a momentary panic washed over me. I lowered my eyes, pretending to be fascinated by something on the ground, just as he stepped over my still stretched legs. I stared at his sneakered feet then looked up to find him glaring.

The Puerto Rican boy stopped a few feet away, his back to me. He stood with his legs spread, hands still in his front pockets, I admired his taut, beefy buns. They were the kind that made me want to spread them, expose the puckered asshole, and sink my teeth and tongue into it.

Slowly, he turned. His lips were pursed as he looked down at me. I admired his bulge openly and licked my lips hungrily. My mouth was watering. I wanted desperately to see what the boy was packing. I looked back up at his face and saw the ghost of a wicked, one-sided smile trace his lips.

He paraded back and forth several times, allowing me to get a good look. From the side, his bulging crotch looked bigger and was even more tempting.

Suddenly, he turned to face me and leaned against a steel beam a foot away from my feet. My eyes swept up and down his body, noticing the lean, hard muscles. He glanced down at my crotch and licked his upper lip.

Unable to resist, I pushed my hips forward even more and spread my legs wider. He planted the bottom of his left foot against the steel beam, cupped his basket with his right hand, and squeezed an invitation. I swallowed back my fear, knowing now that it had been unjustified.

Feeling bold and suddenly quite daring, I squeezed my cock with my left hand in response. His left eyebrow arched when he saw the outline of my erection against the shorts, the swollen head protruding through the bottom. He grinned and my blood boiled.

I was drunk from the heat and the sight of him. I would have followed him anywhere, done anything with him. Instead, I sat and watched as he grasped the tab on his zipper. Watching me, he pulled it down slowly. I licked my lips in anticipation, wondering if anybody was watching.

I saw flesh through the open zipper as he reached inside his pants and groped himself. Mesmerized, I watched as he stroked his meat, then whipped his piece out.

I gasped and stared at the beautiful cock he waved at me. It looked to about eight inches long, uncut, and fat. He pulled the foreskin back, exposing the large, bulbous head. It was flushed an angry purple and slick with Rican pre-cum.

My mouth opened and I stuck my tongue out, inviting him to feed me his thick tubesteak. Moving toward me, his cock jerked from side to side. The tip of his cock was inches from my mouth. It throbbed and jumped in the night air. I stuck my tongue out and licked the head. Then I wrapped my fist around the base of his shaft and licked the length of his fuckpole. I bit and slurped on every inch of his meat, then leaned back to admire it, sloppy and dripping with my spit.

"Suck my big, fat *bicho*!" His voice was husky. He reached out, and holding on to the back of my head, pushed me back onto his cock.

My lips parted and the fat dong slid down my throat. I sucked expertly, bobbing my head back and forth. Every once in a while I bit down on his shaft.

I reached into his pants and pulled out his balls, tugging on them with one hand while, with the other, I stroked the length of meat that didn't fit in my mouth.

He started fucking my face; slowly at first, then picking up speed. His low-hanging balls swayed back and forth, slapping my chin. Suddenly, I wanted to feel him up my ass. I wanted to feel him plugging my hole, and I needed it *now*!

I pulled off his slick cock and looked up at him. His eyes were shiny and glassy with lust. He was getting off on watching my lips slide back and forth over his thick shaft.

"Fuck my ass, man! I want to feel your big, fat, Puerto Rican cock plugging my butthole!" My voice was a harsh whisper. He grabbed his cock by the base and slapped me hard across the face with it. Pre-cum dribbled out of his piss slit. I stuck the tip of my tongue out and lapped at the leaking hole, my tongue swirling.

The Puerto Rican boy went down on his knees and one of his hands groped at my cock and balls. He popped the button on my shorts, then pulled on the zipper. I raised my hips so that he could slide them off. My cock sprang and slapped against my belly.

"Nice dick, man. Not as big as mine. Or as fat. But nice." He took me in his hand and sucked my cock into his warm, wet mouth. The sight of this tough-looking Puerto Rican boy sucking on me made my dick throb. I leaned my head back and moaned as he bit down gently at the base of my shaft. His throat muscles squeezed the head as he deep-throated me.

His left hand slowly stroked the length of his thick root, while the right hand played with my balls. His hot breath seared my flesh and I felt a load building as he probed the crack of my ass with his finger. The suction of his mouth and the slurping noises of his lips were adding to my excitement.

"Stop! Stop or I'll shoot!" I whispered into the evening air I grabbed him by the head and pulled him off my cock. He looked up at me, disappointed that he'd been denied of his prize. His eyes were maniacal with lust.

"What did you do that for? I was gonna use your cum for lube."

"I'm sorry. I just didn't wanna cum yet. Not here. We can go to my place. I only live a few stops away."

"Stand up!" He ignored my suggestion.

I stood and stepped out of my shorts. The night breeze blew against my skin.

"Turn around!"

I did as he commanded and his rough hands grabbed my hairless cheeks. He squeezed then pulled them apart, exposing my puckered hole. I felt it squeeze then relax with sexual excitement, as if it were breathing. The boy sighed behind me then pulled my buns apart even more. I could feel his hot breath as he dove in. The tip of his tongue surfed the edges of my butthole, then darted in and out. I moaned and pushed back, wanting to feel the entire length of his tongue inside me. I wiggled my ass up and down, rubbing against his face as his teeth clamped over the swollen entrance and bit.

"Ohhhh, yeah!" I cried out as he worked his spit into me and tongue-fucked my spasming chute. After a few minutes, he replaced his tongue with one of his thick, long fingers. It sank in to the first knuckle, hesitated as if it had met with resistance, then went all the way in. I groaned with delirious pleasure.

"Oh, yeah, baby! Give me more! I want more!"

"Don't worry, man. I'm gonna shove this *pinga* up your ass in a minute." The boy crooned in a sexy voice as he continued to finger my asshole. He inserted another finger inside me, stretching the walls of my rectal sleeve and getting me ready for his meat. Then he pulled out and stood. Placing his right hand on the small of my back, he grabbed the base of his fat prick in with left and teased the spit-sloppy entrance.

"Fuck me already!" I wiggled my ass, pushing back at him.

The Rican boy pressed his bulbous cockhead against my anxious fuckhole and pushed. The tip of his cock slowly stretched me open and a sharp, stabbing pain ripped through me. I clamped my eyes shut and grit my teeth, determined to take him. I thought only of the pleasure I would feel once the pain subsided.

His fat dickhead suddenly plopped into my hole and I gasped. My body broke into a sweat and I prepared myself for the onslaught. This boy was not going to stop until he had his cock all the way in. I spread my legs wider to give him room.

He made a hawking sound in his throat and I first heard, then felt, a glob as it landed smack at the opening of my stretched manhole. He slicked the Puerto Rican spit along the shaft and pushed deeper.

The ripping sensation gradually disappeared and was replaced by a dull throbbing. It grew as he stuffed me full of hard, hot meat. I sighed as inch by agonizing inch, his fuckpole disappeared inside me until I felt the coarse hairs of his pubic patch. I tugged at my cock and it hardened instantly.

"Okay, baby. Do it!" My voice was husky with desire. He placed his hands on my hips and I knew he was ready to fuck.

The Puerto Rican boy slowly pulled his cock out to the tip. Then he plunged it back in with one steady stroke, making me feel every inch. He thrust his juicy fuckpole in and out of my hole, slow and easy, then fast and rough. At times, he thrust wildly, shoving his cock balls deep into my ass and grinding his hips in a circular motion. He had such skill, such finesse, I knew he had been born to fuck ass. He could have made a mint with his cock!

He rammed me for about ten minutes, his shaft pumping in and out. Then he leaned forward and draped his body over mine, pinching my nipples.

"I'm gonna cum!" He moaned while nibbling on my ear. He pulled his torso off me and pounded my ass with a frenzy. "Oh, fuck! I'm gonna shoot inside your tight, white ass! You're gonna take my *leche*, man!"

I stroked my cock faster and held on to the back of the bench with my free hand. He pounded my ass fast and rough, his cock slamming into my raw, abused fuckhole over and over. His balls slapped against mine as they swayed to and fro, while his shaft rubbed my prostate with each forward thrust. I knew it wouldn't be long before I came along with him.

He leaned back suddenly, burying his fuckstick up to the hilt. He came with a long, loud grunt. I felt the underside of his shaft throb as he bathed the walls of my aching rectum with his dickjuice. The sensation sent me reeling, and I came seconds after. My rectal sleeve squeezed and milked the Rican's cock for every last drop of his seed. My ass was still spasming around the thick root inside me when I finally opened my eyes and looked directly across the platform.

Standing on the Manhattan-bound side was the transit cop. His legs were spread apart, cap raked back on his head. He held the nighstick tightly in his left hand while his right stroked mercilessly up and down

96

on his cut shaft. Our eyes locked. His body trembled and his knees seemed to buckle as he threw his head back. His mouth opened in a round, silent "Oh," and the cop silently shot his load.

I eagerly watched the tip of his cock as it squirt. Spurt after spurt of hot, cop sperm was wasted, splattering on the concrete at his feet. The last drop clung and dangled before finally disconnecting with his slit and landing on his shiny, black right shoe. He looked down disapprovingly then across the platform at us.

The transit cop shook his waning erection once then stuffed it back into his pants and zipped up. He walked towards the stairs and climbed the steps, swinging his nightstick from his wrist in a practiced move. The adrenaline pumped in my veins as I realized what was about to happen. His footsteps grew louder as he got to the landing, then crossed over and went down the steps to where we were.

I gasped, not knowing what to do. My asshole was still clenched around the Rican boy's thick, juicy cock. I could feel his load sloshing inside me.

The cop approached us with a cocky swagger, a wicked grin spreading across his face. He walked around us, taking it in from all angles then stopped in front of me. He tugged at his pants leg slightly, then propped his right shoe on the edge of the bench. I looked down at the lone drop of sperm that had splattered on the shiny, black surface.

"Lick, mother fucker!" His voice was deep and resonant.

I lowered my head, opened my mouth and stuck my tongue out. I lapped at the semen and covered the surface of his shoe for good measure.

"You guys could go to jail for this, you know." He reached out with his right hand, grabbed the back of my head and rubbed his crotch all over my face. I inhaled deeply, smelling his musky scent through the material of his pants. "Yup! I should book you two faggots and give you a personal, overnight tour of our local precinct."

"Officer, please! I . . . we . . ." The Puerto Rican boy's cock started to soften.

"Shut up!" The transit cop's bulge started to grow. I looked up at him, reaching for his zipper while he unbuttoned the blue shirt. His nipples winked at me, slick with sweat as he exposed his hairy chest. I reached into his pants and pulled out his raging hard-on. I stared at it a moment. Some of his copjuice still oozed from the piss slit. I opened my mouth and slurped on the head, sucking out the last drop of his seed. He sighed and thrust his cock deeper into my throat.

"Yeah, boy! That's all you need to do. Just let me in on your little party and I'll pretend I didn't see a thing!" The transit cop pulled out of my mouth and walked around to where the Puerto Rican boy stood with his softened cock still up my ass. "Okay, boy, pull out! It's my turn now!" He rapped the nightstick against the boy's smooth, bare buttocks.

The Puerto Rican boy pulled out slowly. His cock made an audible, slurping sound and the transit cop whistled admiringly. "That's some whopper, kid! Now why don't you go and put it in that cocksucker's mouth. He'll clean that puppy right up for ya." He nodded his head towards me.

The Rican fucker stood before me, his prick now half hard and spongy between his legs. I opened my mouth and sucked on his cock, working it down my throat, down to the balls. Almost immediately, blood filled the veins in his thick shaft. He grabbed my head with both hands, wrapping hair around his fingers, and started to fuck my face while he watched the cop behind me.

The transit cop casually shoved three of his fingers into my stretched out hole. They slid home with no problem. I moaned, my mouth full of cock, while he then fingered me cruelly. After a minute or two, he pulled the digits out and wiped them on my bare ass. Then I felt something cold and hard pressing against my fuckhole.

I stopped sucking the monster cock and looked over my shoulder. The cop was shoving his nightstick up my ass. I groaned as several inches of the club slipped inside me. I pushed my ass back, impaling myself on the cop's stick, and took the Puerto Rican dick back into my mouth.

"I'm not so sure I wanna fuck you. You're so stretched out you probably won't even feel it." The transit cop brutally yanked the nightstick out of my ass and replaced it with his cock. With one stroke he plunged in balls deep, embedding himself up to the pubic hairs. He was right. The Rican cock had made me feel fuller.

Suddenly, I wanted another fuck; a rough and brutal one! As if reading my mind, the cop pulled out of my ass. "Okay, *chico*! Get your little *culo* over here and shove that latin *pinga* up this *puta's* ass!"

"Hey, man! How do you know those words?"

"Shut up, fucker! I ask the questions. But I'll tell ya. I used to have a Puerto Rican girlfriend."

Happy with the answer, the Puerto Rican boy pulled out of my mouth and positioned himself behind me. Slick with spit and come from the previous fucking, he pushed and I felt the swollen dickhead press against my asshole. In one stroke, the entire length of his shaft was buried inside me, splitting my buns in two. I nearly screamed from the sudden intrusion, but the cop silenced me. He stuffed his cock in my mouth and leaned over to watch the furious pounding the Puerto Rican fucker was giving me.

"That's it, you little fucker! Split his ass! Fuck the shit outta him!" The transit cop was encouraging, his voice husky with desire. He crooned other obscenities that I couldn't hear because he placed his hands over my ears and fucked my face. After a moment, he pulled out and replacing his cock with the nightstick. I nearly gagged on the very same end he had shoved up my ass.

"Here! Suck on this for a while. I got business at the other end."

The transit cop walked behind the Puerto Rican boy and scrutinized more closely the intense fucking I was receiving. I looked over my shoulder and watched him pull the boy's tee-shirt up. He clamped his teeth over the left nipple and chewed. The boy grit his teeth and sucked his breath in. He let it out in a loud sigh as the cop then went behind him and spread the boy's buns apart.

For just a moment I wished the Rican boy were fucking someone else. I wanted to see the cop reaming his hole. I looked down between my legs but all I could see was the cop's chin behind the boy's balls.

The boy moaned as the cop thrust a finger up his chute. I could tell that he wasn't accustomed to getting fucked. And yet, he never skipped a beat in his rhythm. He continued to pound my ass mercilessly. His body was slick with night sweat and his skin glistened. He looked so hot behind me, his monster shaft fucking my ass while the cop fingered him. I nearly came, but I wrapped my fist around the base of my shaft and squeezed tight to keep from coming.

The cop ate the boy's hole some more, then stood up after a few minutes, positioning himself behind the boy. I braced myself against the bench, knowing full well that I would be baring the brunt of it all now.

The transit cop pressed forward, pushing into the tight hole before him. The Rican boy registered the intrusion, pain etching itself onto his face. He bit his lower lip, refusing to cry out. Then he slumped forward and rested his body on mine, waiting for the cop to penetrate him fully.

When the cop was all the way inside him, the dark skinned boy stood up again. His cock had gone soft, but I manipulated it with my ass muscles and it began to harden.

The cop pulled his cock out to the tip, then slowly slid it back in. The boy sighed deeply. He thrust backward, pulling me along.

"Give me that!" The cop reached over and took the nightstick from me. I wrapped a fist around my cock and stroked, relishing the monster meat swelling and throbbing to its full proportions inside me. I reached between my legs and grabbed the Puerto Rican's balls, tugging on them as he thrust in and out of me.

"Okay, boy! Fuck that faggot up the ass and fuck yourself on my cock. I'm just gonna stand here!" I looked over my shoulder and watched the incredible sight.

The cop, standing with his shirttails open and out of his pants, leaned back so his cock was halfway out of the boy's hole. As the Puerto Rican boy pushed his cock into me, the cop's cock came almost all the way out; when he pulled out of me, the cop's cock was buried to the hilt up his latin hole. And by the look on his face, I could tell he was enjoying himself. I envied him momentarily.

While the Rican boy fucked me and himself on the cop's cock, I watched the man shove the nightstick into his mouth. He slicked it up with his spit, sucking on it as if it were a big, shiny black cock. He pulled it out, then shoved it up his own ass. The sight of the cop screwing himself with his own nightstick up his ass pushed me over.

"I can't hold back anymore! I'm gonna cum!" I cried out.

A spasm ripped through me as the first spurt erupted. I shivered uncontrollably, my eyes darting from my shooting cock, to the Puerto Rican boy ramming his juicy fuckstick up my ass and fucking himself on the transit cop's manpole, to the cop plunging the nightstick up his own ass. I felt the rectal muscles of my channel clenching and squeezing the shaft fucking me. The Rican's boy's cock throbbed as I milked him.

"*Shit*! I'm gonna cum, too!" He drove his shaft deep, making squishing noises as he came. His second load mingled with the previous one and I could feel his cockjuice dribbling from my raw, and very sore, fuckhole.

Convulsions then swept through the cop's body. Just as the Rican boy came, the cop groaned. His cock spurt deep inside the boy, filling him with his seed. It was one continuous flow of sperm starting with me and ending with the transit cop.

The cop pulled out and walked around to me. He turned, spread his cheeks for me and shoved his asshole onto my face. I reamed him without question.

The Puerto Rican boy pulled out of my ass and walked in front of the cop. He knelt before the man and sucked his sperm-covered cock, tasting his ass on it and cleaning it up. After a moment, he stood and the cop pulled himself together while the Puerto Rican boy stood before me and shoved his cock back into my mouth. I slobbered over his meat, enjoying the taste of my ass and his dickjuice.

When the cop was fully dressed, he went behind the boy and dropped to his knees. Burying his face in the beefy buns, he sucked some of his cum out of the just fucked hole. He swallowed as he stood, licking his lips like a greedy pig.

"Now get dressed. Both of you! And hurry it up! I think I hear the train coming." The cop slapped the boy on the ass with his nightstick then winked at me. Whistling, he started for the stairs.

The Puerto Rican pulled his cock out of my mouth and shot me a smile as he dressed. "That was a wicked fuck! Nobody ever took my dick all the way up their ass before! Did you like it?"

"Like it? I fucking *loved* it!" I pulled my shorts on.

"Think maybe you'd like to get fucked again?"

"Fuck, yeah!" I zipped up, then wiped the sweat and spit off my face with my forearms. "I'm just a little sore right now, though." I walked to the edge of the platform in time to see the train whooshing into the station.

Hot air blew as the train pulled in and came to a stop. The doors flew open and I got on. I turned and stared at the Puerto Rican stud who had just deposited two loads of cream inside me. He stood on the platform, legs spread apart, arms folded on his chest. I looked down at the bulging crotch and felt my cock begin to harden again as I envisioned the different positions he could fuck me in. I jerked my head at him.

The boy rushed forward and stepped into the car just as the doors started to close. He barely made it.

We looked around. There was no one in the car but us.

He sat down, spreading his legs wide open. Thrusting his hips forward, he invited me to unzip him. He smiled wickedly. "We got far to go?"

"Just a couple of stops," I replied.

"Good! Then we have some time. Get on your knees, *puto*!"

Gladly, willingly, I crouched down on my knees between his legs and unzipped him. He didn't have to tell me twice!

# The Writing On The Wall

Sitting on the toilet of the fourth floor college men's room, I looked at the blank wall to my left and realized that it needed something. It was way too bland and boring! I pulled out the marker I kept in my shirt pocket, for just such occasions, and uncapped it. I thought for barely a moment before I started writing.

*Hot, horny, 20 y.o. college student with 7 cut inches good .looks, great body, seeks same for good times. Make me lick your big, fat cock!*

*There, that's better!* I thought as I capped the marker and slipped it back into my shirt pocket. I read what I had just written and wondered what responses I would get. No doubt stuff like: *Go fuck your mother, faggot!* Or, *You oughta be strung up and fucked with a red-hot poker!* Or perhaps a religious one like, *God will see all you homos burn in hell!*

I'd gotten some of those responses in the past; but I didn't care about them. What turned me on was that sometimes men actually communicated back and forth on these walls, leaving hot, dirty messages for every one to witness. It turned me on, too, fantasizing that some guy had gotten off and shot a load in the bowl over the graffiti he was reading; writing on the wall that I had started!

As I sat there, I thought back to the best response I'd gotten, sparked by a message I scrawled on the wall in a high school bathroom during my senior year three years ago.

**They call me Dongo! 12 inches of meat to choke you. Enough milk to drown you. Tomorrow. 3:30 p.m.**

I had gone home, wondering who had written that response; student? teacher? janitor? Perhaps some jock or geeky nerd living out his fantasy of being master. The possibilities were endless and that night I jerked off three times, thinking about who it might be.

The following day, I could barely contain myself as I went from class to class, anxiously awaiting the end of the school day. Classes would be done by three, and a lot of the teachers were there later, but most of the students were gone within 10 minutes of classes ending. No one lingered unless they belonged to a club that met after school, or were part of a sports team.

I had walked around most of the day with a half hard on, my cock ready to stand at attention at the slightest wind. I almost went to the bathroom to jerk off a couple of times that day, but I refrained. I wanted to save it.

And then classes were over.

I lingered in the school library, the final half hour agonizingly slow. At 3:25 I thrust all my books back into my back pack and left the library, my heart tripping loudly through my brain.

*What would I find? Who would be there?* I wondered. My knees felt weak, like rubber; but I pushed on.

My panic was nearly immeasurable as I stood outside the door to the boy's room. I hesitated a moment, one hand on the cool metal. From inside, I heard voices mumbling. Something told me to run, to flee and never look back. But if I did that, I would always wonder. Besides, what did it matter? They would never know what I was there for! All I had to do was stand in front of the urinal or go to a different stall if things looked suspicious when I walked in.

I swallowed loudly and pushed the door open slightly.

Four of the school's biggest goons were in there; all of them trouble makers. And I had fantasized about all of them. They used to walk around with huge, obscene bulges, obviously placing great pride in what was to them, and me, the most important aspect of their maleness; their cocks.

The four big boys stood in the middle of the bathroom, laughing and talking, adjusting their crotches. But the one that caught my eye was Timothy Kelly, captain of the football team. He stood there smoking, which wasn't allowed, arms crossed, his ass leaning against the sink. His long legs were crossed at the ankles and when the door opened, he cast a sideways glance to see who was coming in.

As hard as my cock was, and as bad as I wanted them, I took a step back, letting the door slam shut. The noise got their attention and from outside I heard one of them yell. "He's here! Let's get the little faggot and fuck his ass!"

Terrified, my heart pounding, I managed to make a quick getaway through a nearby exit. They had not seen me, so I knew I would be safe.

But I always regretted and fantasized about the gangbang that could have been.

I saw myself down on my knees before them, forced to suck each one off and swallow their young loads. They would have watched while I knelt in front of The Captain, in front of Tim, and deep throat his butt-rammer. After swallowing his load, they would have pulled me up off the floor, ripped my clothes off and push me up against a stall partition. One of the goons would have gotten on his knees, spread my buns apart and spit in my hole. He would have gotten up, run his hand through his greasy hair, and used it to lube his cock. And then he would have put the head up against my tight fuckhole and pushed. He would have split me open and fucked me until he shot a load up my ass. Then the others would have taken their turn; each time my hole getting looser and sloppier.

Just as I was about to get to the part in my fantasy where Tim was going to fuck me, I shot my load, oozing slowly out of my piss slit.

II wiped myself off, pulled my pants up and left the bathroom, leaving the freshly written graffiti and the load of cum to fester on the wall.

I checked the stall nearly every day for a week. I had incited a riot, where nothing but clean, blank space existed before! A proliferation of smut and an equal amount of political garbage had blossomed. But it was the smut that interested me.

One guy wanted to drip melting wax on my nipples while he whipped my cock and balls with a leather strap. Another wanted me to piss all over his body, and yet another said he liked to dress up in women's clothes while a real butch man rode him like a horse.

But there was only one response that truly caught my attention.

*They call me Dongo. Where and when, cocksucker?*

I was so turned on I jerked off right then and there. I shot a load that sprayed all over the messy wall. The janitor was going to have fun cleaning that one up! Then I replied.

*Day after tomorrow. 3:30. Here.*

I was a nervous wreck the next couple of days, reminded of that afternoon in high school. Since then, I had met a few guys in the same fashion and they had all turned out to be total disasters. Although terrified that this one would turn out the same, I was still aroused. My curiosity would not allow me to chicken out!

When the time came, I went into the bathroom and sat down in the stall where I had written the message. After a few minutes, the door burst open and a man shuffled to the stall beside mine. My heart pounded and I would have sworn it could be heard throughout the entire floor; if not the entire building.

I held my breath and turned my head to look at the man's feet. He had dropped his pants and boxer shorts. From what little I could see of his thin legs, the skin looked yellow, the hair on them sparse. Then an orchestra of farts broke the silence in the bathroom. I heard him take a piss, then a dump, and after a few minutes, he left.

I was relieved.

I waited another ten minutes. Then, all of a sudden, the door opened. Someone stood in front of the urinal. I heard a zipper then I saw a floppy black cock with uncut skin, through the slit in the stall.

I wondered.

Shortly after that, the door opened again and a second man went into the stall one over from mine.

I gulped, thinking, what if this was now a trap? Thugs? School security? Police?

The door opened shortly thereafter and a third man walked in. He took the only other stall available. The one directly next to me.

I gulped nervously, suddenly feeling I had made a huge mistake.

But then the man at the urinal left and I breathed a bit easier.

After a few more minutes, the guy in the far stall audibly finished his business and stormed out without washing his hands. I was disgusted at the thought but relieved.

It was down to me and the man in the stall next to me.

I looked down at the man's sneakered feet. As I looked down, he spread his legs apart a little and brought his left foot closer. Then he cleared his throat.

This was him! I was sure of it! I had looked forward to meeting him and finding out who he was, but now I didn't know what to do. I was paralyzed. It was so quiet in the bathroom I could hear my wristwatch ticking. I looked at it: 4:10.

*Fuck! I'm late for class! What the hell was I doing?!*

The man in the next stall cleared his throat again and, without thinking, so did I. Then the roll of toilet paper in his stall rattled on its spindle. A second later a sheet of white paper fluttered to the floor on my side. Thinking maybe there was something written on it, I picked it up; it was blank.

The roll of toilet paper rattled again and I heard him rip off another square. This time, I heard the click of a pen and waited. The second piece of toilet paper fell to the floor and I picked it up.

*You want my hard cock up your ass or in your mouth?*

My heart tripped in my chest, the blood pumping loudly in my head. I pulled out a pen and responded.

*Both! But I'm a little nervous.*

I let the piece of toilet paper flutter back to the floor. A large hand with thick, long fingers picked it up.

*Don't be. Let's get outta here? Too many people.*
*But I should warn you. They call me Dongo.*

Every nerve in my body twitched from excitement and fear. I stood, pulled my pants up, and heard him do the same. He slid the bolt on his door and stepped out of the stall. I remained in mine a moment, took a deep breath, then let it out slowly. Reaching for the bolt, I slid it back and opened the door.

My jaw nearly dropped to the floor. For a moment, I thought I was dreaming; but it was real. Standing in front of the sink, washing his hands, was Timothy Kelly. He looked at me and stared me in the eye. I thought I saw a twinkle of recognition as a crooked smile broke across his face. Instantly, my dick stiffened.

Timothy Kelly stood a little under six feet, his body hard muscle. His wide shoulders captivated me, and I thought, *My ankles would look great perched there.*

His large biceps stretched the short sleeves of the white, knit pull-over he wore, emblazoned with the school name across the front. The material molded to his expansive chest and well-developed pecs, while stiff nipples thrust out against the cloth like bicycle tire valves. I bit my lower lip, imagining myself licking, biting, and chewing on them while he pounded my ass.

The material of his faded blue jeans clung invitingly to his thick thighs and beefy, bubble butt. I saw myself spreading his buns apart and burying my tongue in the sweaty crack as he sat on my face. Then he turned to face me and my eyes went down to the bulging basket. I nearly swooned.

"So what do you think? Interested?" His voice was husky and low. I looked up into his eyes and could only nod. "Good. You got a place we can go? I gotta drop a load soon or I'm gonna rape you right on the spot." Timothy Kelly clutched at his bulge and squeezed it. I licked my lips, wondering briefly if I wasn't getting in over my head.

"Wanna go to my dorm room?" I asked. A part of me wished he would make good on his threat.

"Lead the way." I could feel Tim's eyes taking me in from head to toe.

"By the way, I'm Johnny." I thrust my hand out at him. He took it in his and squeezed hard. The energy coursing through his hand nearly burned me.

"I know," he replied with a smirk. "We went to the same high school. I remember you."

"You do?" I was surprised. I didn't think high school jocks ever paid attention to book nerds.

"Yeah. Some of us do. I'm Tim."

"I . . . I know. I remember you from the football team."

"Okay, a little less talkee so we can go fuckee!" Tim motioned and nudged me towards the door. He stepped aside as I walked past him. One of his hands reached out and cupped my ass hard. I nearly dropped to my knees with desire.

We were both silent during the short walk to my dorm room. Once inside, Tim closed and locked the door behind him. I sat down at the foot of the bed and he stood before me. I looked at his bulging crotch, growing ever bigger, then looked up at him, feeling lost all of a sudden.

"Whassamatter?" Tim asked. I shook my head. He smiled. "You're probably thinking to yourself maybe you got in over your head?" I nodded and he chuckled.

"Well, maybe you did." He reached out and grabbed the back of my head, forcing my face into his groin. I loved the rough feel of denim and his throbbing mound against my face.

While he peeled off his shirt, I unzipped his jeans. I ran my tongue over his belly and reached inside to pull out his ample cock. I grabbed it by the base and stared at it for a moment; it was huge and thick and heavy in my hand. He certainly had not advertised falsely!

I stuck my tongue out and licked the length of his shaft. Then, overpowered by the wicked, almost animalistic power emanating from him, I devoured the bulbous cockhead. I reached for the huge ball sac and squeezed as I slid my mouth along the length of his thick meat and bit down. Tim growled.

Sucking on Tim's cock, he reached down and unbuttoned my shirt. He tweaked at my nipples, pinching them hard. I moaned, my mouth full of cock.

"Like that?" Tim whispered. I moaned my reply. "Just wait. We're gonna do things you'll enjoy even more."

"Like what?" I asked, talking around his cock. Tim smacked me gently upside the head. I looked up at him, stunned, but not scared.

"Didn't your mother tell you not to speak with your mouth full?" I nodded. "For starters, I'm gonna eat your hole, Johnny. You're gonna love it, too. I've got a big, long tongue just made for rimming." He opened his mouth and made lewd gestures with his tongue, the way Gene Simmons from KISS used to do. I moaned, my eyes opening wide at the thought of Tim's tongue on my hole, probing me deeply.

"Then, I'm gonna fuck that pretty little ass of yours. Fuck it 'til you burn. Spread you apart with my thick tool." He grabbed the back of my head and started to pump his cock in and out of my mouth; more than three quarters of it remained unserviced because of its length. But that would soon change.

After a moment, Tim pulled his cock out of my mouth and took the rest of his clothes off. I stood up and did the same. My own, average-sized cock, which I thought was a good size, looked small compared to his. I found it intimidating, but he didn't even notice my hard-on.

"Get on the bed," Tim growled. "On your back, head hanging over the side."

I did as he said and watched as Tim walked up to me, his cock bobbing pendulously as he straddled my head. His cock dangled just before my lips.

"Open your mouth. Wide. Wider!" I did as he commanded and he brought the head of his cock to my waiting face hole. Then, slowly, the entire length of his thick, juicy bat was pumped into my mouth and down my throat. I gagged at first, but then I relaxed and my throat muscles rippled against his cockhead. Tim moaned, leaned forward on his hands and started to fuck my mouth in earnest. Tears welled in my eyes and my cheeks puffed out with every thrust.

After a few minutes of steady throat pounding, I was choking, my breath erratic. I felt like I would pass out. Snot was snorting and bubbling out from my nose and spittle flew everywhere. And yet I didn't want him to stop. If I had to die from asphyxiation at least his was the cock that I wanted to be choked by.

"That pussy mouth feels good, Johnny!" Tim moaned. "I love your teeth scraping my cockflesh, my balls banging on your face. You like my cock fucking your mouth?" All I could do was nod; I didn't dare attempt to speak. Tim's cock wiggled inside my throat and we both moaned. "I'm gonna shoot my load all over your pretty little face. You wanna see it?" Tim started to pull his cock out of my mouth.

But I reached out and held on to the round, firm globes that were his ass.

"So you wanna swallow it, huh?" I could almost feel the smirk on Tim's face as he slid his pole back into place. "I'll cum down your throat, pig. Only cause you begged for it."

I moaned as Tim started to pump in and out of my mouth. His cock throbbed, then, suddenly, he pulled out. He grabbed his spit shined cock and pumped it. I watched as it loomed menacingly above me and whimpered, having been denied of what I wanted most.

Tim cried out, his body spasming, while the first spurt ripped through him. My greedy mouth flew open, trying to wrap my lips around the head of his dick, but he was just out of reach. The rest of his load squirted out in big globs and he grunted, groaning like a wounded animal as he squirt his load on my face. And all I could do was stick my tongue out, my eyes wide open because I didn't want to miss the sight of his cock erupting. I moaned along with him as a couple of drops landed on my tongue and I nearly swooned with the flavor of him.

As his orgasm subsided, Tim slipped the head of his cock back into my mouth and I whimpered like a puppy, sucking greedily, enjoying the taste of his sperm bursting on my tongue. I stroked my cock as I lapped at Tim's cockhead, savoring his dick milk. I let out a muffled cry and shot my own load. It spurt through the air, landing on my belly in thick drops.

Tim pulled his cock from my mouth and picked up the first thing he could find; my underwear.

"Wipe your face," he said and threw them at me. I sat up in bed and did as he asked. Then Tim pushed me back and draped his entire body over mine. He kissed me, hot and demanding, his tongue forcing its way into my mouth.

Tim scooted down between my legs and wrapped a hand around the base of my hard prick. He started to stroke it and I thought he was about to suck me. But I should have known better.

Anxious for the hole he had claimed as his own, Tim flipped me over onto my stomach and spread my cheeks apart. He buried his face between my musky smelling buns, and his tongue found my hairless, puckered chute. I felt myself melt against him as his tongue probed further, plunging deeper into the pink rosebud that would soon be his. I reached behind me in desperation, grabbing at the back of his head, pushing him in deeper.

Tim pulled away from my fuckhole and I looked over my shoulder to watch as he spit into the palm of his hand and smeared it all over the head of his huge cock, the length of his meat. He grabbed my cheeks again, spread them, and spit several times onto my hole. Stroking his cock with one hand, he worked the spit into the rectal sleeve with two fingers. The sheer size of his meat made my head reel and for a moment I panicked. It had been a while since I'd been fucked and I wondered if I could take him.

My butthole clenched around his two fingers, but Tim released his prick, slapped me hard on the ass and hoarsely urged me to relax.

"I don't know, man. That thing is really big!"

"Fuck you, man! You got me hard and excited. And you're gonna get fucked!"

I moaned and closed my eyes as he continued to work my hole.

"Yeah, baby. That's it. Relax that fuckhole. This bad boy is gonna bury itself deep inside you."

I put my head back down, delirious with his words, and the sensation that had overcome my body. It was as if reasoning and practicality had been thrown out. The only thing that existed, or mattered, was the burgeoning sensation that flowed from my asshole, still spasming around his fingers, spreading through the rest of my body. I was one nerve, one sensation; the sensation of blind, wanton desire. I wanted him and I wanted him badly. I wanted him to possess me, empower me, and completely engulf me, piercing me with the thickness of his 12 inch cock!

I felt him pull his fingers out and replace them with the tip of his cock. It pressed against my hole, hot and burning, like a hot poker. He pushed and my tight, barely used chute started to open and accept the thick mushroom head of his cock. Even with the intense tonguing he'd given me and the spit-lube job, the pain was intense. My asshole felt like it was going to rip.

"Wait! No, please! It hurts too much! Take it out for a minute!"

"No, way! You wanted to get fucked? You're gonna get fucked. Now shut up and take it like a man!"

"But . . . I hardly ever . . . it's been a long time since . . ."

"I really don't care," Tim grunted and roughly shoved my head down into the mattress. At the same time, he thrust his cock inside me. He pushed. And kept pushing.

I felt as if I were about to pass out from the incredible pain and the lack of oxygen. My brain was telling my body to push it out, to fight it, fight him, but my asshole knew what it wanted. I screamed into the mattress, tears in my eyes from the pain and humiliation. And yet, I pushed out as I were taking a shit.

After a moment, he released the pressure on the back of my head With agonizingly slow steadiness, my ass lips opened up to accept the girth of meat he was giving me. I reached between us and felt my asshole, sucking on his shaft. I wrapped my fingers around him and felt upwards toward his groin. He had about half of his meat inside me and that was all I needed. The frenzied desperation hit me again.

I moaned and started to push up against him as he struggled to push down into me.

Tim snickered and threw the entire weight of his body on top of me, pinning me down. He held my outstretched arms while the sweat on my back mixed with the sweat from his smooth, hairless chest. I whimpered as he nudged another inch of meat up my ass.

"Relax." He tried to soothe me and thrust another couple of inches inside me. I yelped and he bit down at the base of my neck. I crooned and he thrust yet another inch into me. "You got almost all of it inside you, now." Tim grunted. I swooned as the remaining inches of the monster meat impaled me.

He groaned, the last remaining inches firmly entrenched and deeply buried inside my raw fuckhole. He lay panting on top of me. "There you go, baby. It's all inside you, now."

I sighed with disbelief from the sheer size of him and closed my eyes, feeling my cock harden once more. I couldn't believe I had taken the entire length of his shaft. The pain was still there, slowly ebbing away, but it was being replaced by rough-edged pleasure that mixed with the pain. And it was intoxicating.

Tim lay still on top of me for another moment and then slowly started to move his hips. I moaned with wicked desire as the sensations that coursed through my body possessed me. Tim repositioned himself, balancing his weight on his hands on either side of me. Slowly, he pulled out of me until only the tip was left. I could just about feel the ridge of his cockhead pulling against the lips of my stretched and abused fuck hole. But they held on tight, sucking on the head of his meat. Then he plunged and buried the entire length of his hot shaft balls deep inside me. I screamed out, loving the way his hips slammed against me, grinding deeper and deeper.

Tim pounded me, his hips at times a blur, like a battering ram, pistoning in and out of me. Then he corkscrewed his groin against my backside, the tip of his cock pushing deeper and further than anything had ever been before. His dickhead rubbed my prostate every time he pushed in and pulled out. For nearly half an hour, Tim plowed my hole and when he couldn't hold back any longer, he buried his fuckstick deep in my ass and grunted into my ear loudly, pushing me further into the mattress. I couldn't breath as the creamy spunk from his balls shot through the length of his shaft and filled my raw, red, and abused rectum.

I relished the throbbing that coursed through me; first from his cock, then through my stretched out fuck chute, and finally to the rest of my body. The heat of his manseed pushed me over the edge and I cried out along with him.

My balls churned as a second load ripped through me, and we lay perfectly still for what seemed an eternity. We might have even fallen asleep. I'm not sure. When you're fucked like that, by such a big piece of meat, time stands still. And yet it seems to stretch on into forever. The endorphins tripping through my body made me feel as if I were high.

When our breathing had abated, I felt myself coming back to consciousness.

"You okay?" He lay on top of me still. I nodded. "That was incredible." Tim muttered in my ear, his voice low and husky. Once again I nodded. I was speechless. "Tell me something." Tim continued. "Why did you run?"

"What?"

"That afternoon. In high school? I knew it was you."

"How? Why didn't you ever say anything?" But Tim didn't respond. I finally shrugged. "I guess I was scared."

"Scared of little ole me?" I could feel his cock beginning to harden again inside me.

"I was scared you were all gonna kick the living shit outta me and leave me in some corridor to be found by the janitor."

"Or maybe you were just scared you'd enjoy it too much?" Tim suggested. "You would have loved it, you know," Tim said, stroking my belly. "You missed out on some great fucking!"

"Oh, I don't know. I think I just got some of it."

"I guess we're just gonna have to make up for lost time. Whaddaya think? Wanna be my bitch?"

I didn't have to think about it. I nodded eagerly and we both smiled.

"C'mon! I wanna feel my cum shooting deep inside you again. But this time, you're gonna ride it!" Tim pushed up off me and started to pull his hardening meat out of me. The pain started to course through me once again. "Breathe deep." I did as he asked me. "Now let it out slowly." And as I responded, I felt him slipping out of me. It felt like I was taking the best shit of me life! Incredible slow and nearly ecstatic with pleasure, he came away with a loud slurping sound. I felt my asshole clamp shut with an audible farting sound. But it didn't phase either one of us.

Tim lay back, an arm behind his head, waving his thick, long shaft in the air at me. He held it by the base and all I could do was stare at it in amazement. That monster meat had worked its way inside me and fucked me raw. But what was more amazing, was that I wanted it again, used as my hole felt, stretched as my insides were. I didn't care.

I climbed on top of him, straddling his hips. The head of his cock found my hole. I held the shaft, my hand just above his own and relaxed my hole as the thick mushroom head lodged itself. I sat down slowly, my stretched boyhole, now a manhole, yielding as I pressed further.

We grunted and groaned together, lost in our own world of pleasure while I sat down further and he plunged upward, thrusting his entire length balls deep inside me.

I thought of all the wasted time between high school and now. All that time I could have had him. But, of course, he was right. We were simply going to have make up for lost time.

I just hoped my asshole could last that long!

# The Donatellos

I was a senior in high school when the Donatellos moved into the house next door in the spring of 1976. I was the youngest of three sons and the last to leave home.

I didn't really notice them at first; I was busy with my upcoming graduation, winning swim tournaments for school, and running around town trying, unsuccessfully, to get my rocks off, fuck some pussy, and tongue some tit. Looking back, it seems that was all I ever wanted to do. What else is there for a horny young athlete with a big cock? Dick action, regardless of what kind, is all we're good for. Unfortunately for me, I had not yet discovered the pleasures of uninhibited sex with a woman. It was only my palm that created friction between it and my cock, balls bouncing, endless streams of cum shooting and drying on my belly. In my fantasies, however, I'd done it all.

Mom did the June Cleaver thing and baked the Donatellos a cake to welcome them to the neighborhood. Dad invited them over for a Memorial Day weekend barbecue, to which it seemed the entire block had been invited as well.

That was where I finally met Joey and Angela.

Joey Donatello was one of those swarthy, good-looking Italian men that reek of masculinity and virility. He was nearly six feet tall and dark haired; a thick mustache like a paint brush, and a perpetual four o'clock shadow on his face. He had deep set brown eyes that were so dark they were almost black. His body was well defined, but not excessively built.

"This is my son, Johnny." Dad introduced me. "Son, this is Mister Donatello from next door. He's in construction."

"Honey?" Mom cried out from across the lawn. "I think the burgers are burning!"

"Shit, woman! Just flip them over!" Dad shouted, but trotted away towards the grill.

"So! How yuh doin'?" Our new neighbor asked politely. His voice was deep and husky, with just a slight hint of a Brooklyn accent. He extended his hand and I took it in mine. His grip was hard and firm. I squeezed back and felt an odd, curious tingle creep up my arm. Goosebumps broke out over the back of my neck and up my arms. I looked up at him and stared into his eyes. There seemed to be an amused, playful smirk of a smile on his face.

"It's a pleasure meeting you, Mr. Donatello," I replied, refusing to be shaken by the strange feeling that suddenly came over me.

"Please, call me Joey," he said. "Everybody does. Mister just sounds so . . . *old*."

"Okay then, Joey," I said nervously, and watched him grin, slowly and suggestively.

"Your dad tells me your quite the athlete," Joey commented.

"Dad's been talking again, huh?" I let out a nervous chuckle, uncomfortable with the art of small talk; especially with him. "I'm on the baseball and swim teams. But swimming is what I'm really good at. I've won several awards for school."

"So I hear. Your dad must be very proud of you," Joey said softly, teasing. "If my son was a good looking star athlete, I'd wanna talk about him, too!"

"Oh! You have kids?"

"No, not yet. My wife and I have been enjoying our honeymoon."

"Ah, so you're newlyweds!"

Joey laughed a deep, hearty laugh. "Naw, not really. I just like to say that. We've been married five years, now."

"I don't understand." Joey just smiled and leaned toward me. I felt his hot breath in my ear as he whispered, his lips and tongue far too close for my comfort; yet I did not move.

"We like to fuck a lot. Know what I mean?"

"I wouldn't know," I responded without thinking, trying to avoid his gaze; but I couldn't seem to help myself. He had the kind of smile that made women want to throw their panties at him and spread their legs willingly. In his eyes was a look that implied much raw sensuality. I tried to understand what was happening to me, why I was feeling the way I was, and why all of a sudden I wanted to have his lips and tongue on my neck. I'd never felt that way before, least of all for a man. I found it oddly disturbing, yet strangely titillating. I wondered briefly why it was that I suddenly had visions of him naked.

He leaned toward me once more. I leaned in, too, longing to feel his hot breath again, unable to resist my conflicting emotions. "Why does a handsome jock like you not know about fucking? I mean, I've seen you swimming in your pool. Your Speedos don't exactly hold anything back, you know. I would have thought you'd have more than your fair share of pussy," he explained.

I pulled away from him feeling a hot flush creep up my neck and face. Joey smiled seductively, as if he took great pride in unnerving me. All I could do was shrug.

"I'll have to fix you up with this girl I know." Joey winked, clamped a big hand on my shoulder and squeezed it tight. I gulped as my knees grew weak suddenly and a hot rush of warmth spread throughout my body. I knew then my cock had just leaked some precum.

"Excuse me," I said, taking a step away from him.

"You all right?" He asked, appearing suddenly concerned. "You look kinda pale."

"Hi, honey!" A voice chimed out of nowhere. I turned to see a petite woman come up beside him with two bottles of beer. She handed one of them to him and he took it, wrapping thick, long fingers around the neck as if he were holding up his cock.

I swallowed hard as I drank in the sight of her ample breasts hugged by the snug tee-shirt she wore. Her nipples were hard and poked through the thin material. I knew in that instant she would not make very many friends among the married women of the neighborhood. The men, however, married or not, would be a different story. I glanced around and found proof of my hunch. Several of the men stood together, drinking beer and talking to one another, sneaking peaks at her from behind. One of them said something that made another chuckle, shake his head, and walk off toward his wife.

"Hi, babe." Joey wrapped an arm around her shoulders and squeezed her to him. He planted a kiss on the top of her head. "Johnny, this is my wife, Angela. Angela, this is Johnny." He lifted the bottle to his mouth, took a long, large swig and swallowed melodramatically.

"Pleased to meet you," she said, never taking her eyes off me. I extended my hand and she took it in hers. The skin was soft, and, just like her husband, her touch made my skin crawl excitedly, tingling with goose bumps. I don't think I was subtle as my eyes swept from her long, wavy, brown hair -- that I would have liked to jerk off with and use to whip her head up and down on my shaft -- to her small, pouty red lips, which I thought would look delicious wrapped around the base of my hard prick, stretching to accommodate my thickness. I briefly wondered how Joey was hung.

An image of the two of them, naked and entwined, tangled amidst bed sheets, suddenly burned itself into my brain. I could see them wrestling in my mind's eye, and another sudden rush of warmth swept through me; I knew I had leaked again. I could feel the precum oozing out of my piss slit and I knew I had to get off soon; otherwise I'd keep on leaking and would soon start to show a wet spot on my cut-off shorts.

"It was certainly a pleasure meeting you, Johnny," Joey said, as if he could read my mind. "I have a feeling we're gonna be great friends."

"I'd like that." I replied nervously, unsure of what might happen if we were.

"Nice meeting you." Angela said, and I nodded in her direction. I turned around and started walking, trying not to appear as though I was anxious to get away. I didn't know which one I would fantasize about first; perhaps I would think of both! And underneath it all, was my disturbed curiosity as to why I felt the way I did when Joey whispered in my ear and squeezed my shoulder. I had never felt that way before! I had never even thought about men, until I met him! I wondered how that could be as I walked into the house and up to my room.

Inside, I walked across my bedroom and looked out the window. I could see them from where I was, standing together, still talking. She said something to him and he seemed to think for a moment; then he shrugged. She wrapped her arms around his waist and stood on the tips of her toes. He leaned down, and from where I stood, I could see his tongue probe her mouth. He pulled her toward him and squeezed her, still holding the bottle of beer. I couldn't wait to hear what the gossip around the neighborhood would be after this weekend barbecue; just as I could no longer wait to free my throbbing, leaking, stiffening prick.

I tugged at my cut-offs, an old pair of 501s worn thin from much wear and tear. Reaching into my white jockey briefs, I hauled out my cock and floppy balls. The elastic waistband pushed my balls up against my cock and made them look bigger than they were. I liked the way they looked spreading on either side of my thick cock. I wrapped my fingers around the middle of my shaft and stroked it, filled with great pride over the size I had been blessed with. Fully hard, I was 8 1/2 inches. Around the base I was a little over 4 1/2 inches thick, and the head, large and purple, was nearly five.

A clear, viscous strand of juice oozed out of the piss slit and dangled like liquid thread. With the tip of my finger, I swabbed it against the red, throbbing head of my cock and rubbed the slick juice between my thumb and forefinger. Having tasted it before, I found myself craving it. I stuck the two fingers in my mouth and sucked at them greedily. The salty tang of my own juices only increased my thirst. I fisted my cock roughly to pump more juice out of my balls, then, slowly and tightly, squeezed down toward the angry, purplish-red head; it reminded me of a stewed tomato.

Another, longer strand of cock juice oozed out of my piss slit and I fingered it hungrily. Sucking at the finger in my mouth, I squeezed my cock and stroked it up and down roughly, almost abusively. I closed my eyes as I imagined that perhaps it was Joey's cock, thick, huge and Italian, throbbing in my mouth, while Angela wrapped her pink lips around the head of my dick and made me shoot a load on her smooth, dark skin.

My cock throbbed and a familiar feeling gripped my balls. A fiery explosion seemed to take place in my groin and then my dick burst after a few more strokes. I watched the head of my cock as young sperm spluttered against the window pane. My body shivered, my cock still squirting, as I gripped my cock and squeezed it from the base to the head, milking it for every last available drop. In the throes of sexual delirium, I sank to my knees and hungrily lapped at my own sperm, excited beyond anything I could have ever imagined or fantasized.

As I came back to my senses, I realized that anyone looking up might have witnessed what had just taken place. I looked to see if anyone had noticed, but everyone below seemed unaware; they were too busy having a good time and eating barbecue.

And then I noticed Joey Donatello sitting in a lawn chair.

The sun shone down on his rugged, handsome face while he squinted his eyes and looked directly up at my bedroom window. I quickly stepped back, my softening cock spilling a lone drop of come on the window sill. I peered through the curtains, watching him, wondering how long he'd been looking up at me. Had he seen me jerking off? Had he seen me lapping up my own sperm like a hungry dog lapping at a bowl of milk? Or was he merely looking up at the sky? And if he'd seen anything, would he tell my folks? Would he tell his wife? Would he keep it a secret and say nothing? Or would he mention it to me? I found I wanted him to confront me about it. I found I wanted them both, intensely, to watch me. A sudden urge of desire to fuck his wife while I sucked his cock, made me feel bold enough to step to the window again.

Unsure if he could even see, I glared at him while tucking my cock and balls back inside my jockeys. I buttoned my shorts up and cupped my crotch at him, hoping that he was able to see me, yet frightened at the thought of what he would do if he really could.

If he saw me, he gave no indication. He merely looked up at my bedroom window, lifted the bottle of beer up to his lips, and sucked down the remainder of it, guzzling at the amber liquid until it was all gone. He lowered the bottle and smacked his lips, wiping his mouth with his forearm. Then he got up from his chair and disappeared from view.

I stood still for a moment, paralyzed with fear and desire. Where had he gone, what would he do?

"This is ridiculous," I muttered to myself. "He didn't see anything. It's all in your head. And you DON'T like guys! Only fags like guys!" I convinced myself. I walked across the room, though my knees still felt as if they were made of rubber, opened the door and suddenly stopped short.

"Where's your bathroom?" I heard Joey ask my mother, downstairs in the kitchen.

"It's at the top of the stairs, next to Johnny's room."

"Great, thanks! Oh, here, let me carry that for you."

"Oh, no! I've got it. You can hold the door open for me, though." The door opened and closed, and then the house went still and silent.

I peered over the banister from where I was, but I couldn't see much below. I took a step, and just when I was beginning to think he'd left, I heard him clear his throat and walk towards the stairs. I gulped and leaped back into my bedroom. I closed the door quietly, locked it, and leaned my ear against the door. My heartbeat thumped loudly in my head, and my heart jumped up into my throat as I stood there, listening as he took the stairs two at a time.

*What's he going to do?* I wondered and felt myself starting to panic.

With my heart still in my throat, I swallowed loudly as the bathroom door opened. The toilet seat went up noisily and I heard him piss into the bowl for what seemed an eternity. After a while, he flushed, and the seat clattered back into position. Then there was the sound of rushing water as he washed his hands.

I remained at my post, my ear against the door, listening to the silence. I couldn't hear his footsteps. I panicked at the thought of him just standing there in the corridor, coming to my bedroom door.

*Would he really do it?* I wondered and was once again surprised to find that I wanted him to. I wanted him to come to my door, to knock, to open it and step inside. I wanted him to come up to me, lean against me the way he had with his wife and thrust his tongue deep into my mouth as I'd seen him do to Angela.

I didn't know what was happening to me. I didn't know where those feelings had come from, or even why. I only knew that all of a sudden, he had opened something up inside me. His touch had awakened something that began to stir deep within me and his looks had filled my mind with images of thoughts I'd never had before.

A timid knock caught me by surprise, even though I had been willing it to happen. I stepped back, watching the doorknob slowly turn. I'd forgotten that I'd locked the door and found myself too shocked to move.

*Open it, you fool!* A voice hollered inside my head.

The knock came again, this time a bit more sure of itself. And still I did not move.

"Johnny?" His voice came through the door, low, yet deep and resonant. There was a huskiness to it that made me tingle and made my dick twitch inside my pants. But I was still paralyzed with fear and excitement from the thought that just on the other side of that door stood a man that I could let into my room, and under the very roof that I shared with my parents, make me experience all sorts of things.

*Experience what?! Sucking his cock?! Sucking yours?! Jerking off together and who knows what else?! You'd like that, wouldn't you?! Open it! Go ahead!* The voice inside my head seemed to yell and it broke my paralysis.

"Yes, yes," I muttered and stepped towards the door. "Joey?" I called out, and as soon as the question left my mouth I felt foolish. I already knew who it was.

"Yeah, it's me. Open the door," he whispered huskily, his voice making me want to strip off my clothes and let him have his way with me, do whatever he wanted.

Downstairs, the back door opened and I heard my father's laughter at something someone outside had said. "He must be upstairs. I'll just go and see," he volunteered. The door shut behind him. "Johnny?" He called out to me.

"Shit!" I muttered.

On the other side of the door, I could hear Joey step away and start towards the stairs. I bolted for the door and unlocked it. I threw it open and watched as Joey froze to the spot. He turned to look at me, one hand on the rail, a fresh bottle of beer in his other hand. He had one foot on one step and the other on the rise above it. Joey stared at me and I saw him swallow, as if debating which step to take.

I drank in the sight of him, noticing the light sheen of sweat from his own excitement and the sun outside. I looked down at his crotch and thought I saw something growing there, but I couldn't be sure. Out of nervousness, I licked my lips. I would discover much later in life that a lick of the lips suggested promises of oral favors.

Joey turned as he glared at me, his eyes half closed and somewhat glazed. He took a step up the stairs, towards me.

I took a deep breath and stepped back, away from the doorway, as if he were already entering my room and I had no choice but to let him pass.

He took another step up.

The spit in my mouth had dried and my tongue slithered out again, across dry lips, trying to moisten them. I could feel the heat in my groin as it crept up my body, my dick thickening and hardening inside my jockeys yet again.

"Johnny!" My dad cried, louder this time.

I gulped and Joey froze in his steps. Then he smirked and turned his back on me. He went down the stairs just as my dad was coming up.

"Oh, hey, Joey! I was just coming up to see if Johnny was in his room."

"I don't know," he replied. "I was just in the bathroom. Too much beer."

"Yeah." Dad chuckled. "I know what you mean. You know, that wife of yours . . . wow! What a doll! She's a real sweetheart."

"Yeah, she is," Joey said. "I'll tell her you said so. It's always hard meeting people and making new friends when you move into a new neighborhood. Thanks."

"My pleasure. Well, I guess I better go and look for my son. See you outside."

"Yup," Joey said, and descended the stairs. The back door opened and closed.

"Johnny! You up there? The Snyders are here and they want to see you! Johnny?!"

"Yeah! I'm here!" I hollered back at my Dad. "I'll be right down!"

But I didn't feel like seeing anyone or doing anything other than having Joey in my bedroom. I wanted to scream and yell at my dad for having come into the house when he did. I didn't give a shit who had come or who was asking about me. I only knew that I felt empty and extremely disappointed. My body ached and quivered with longing. My cock had made me feel the hope and promise of another body's contact, and until that point, I had not realized how much I had been craving it. Jerking off was fine, but I knew instinctively that nothing would beat the feeling of a warm, hot body pressed up against mine, or a hot mouth around my cock, a hand on my balls, a finger up my ass, or a moist hole riding the length of my shaft.

It seemed from then on, all I did was jerk off thinking about Joey Donatello getting his cock sucked, eating his wife's pussy and chewing on her erect nipples while fucking her; always fucking, plunging and thrusting in my mind.

In bed at night, awake and unable to sleep, I jerked off once and sometimes twice before I finally dozing off. But my cock remained hard, my balls aching from coming so much and wasting all those loads on my belly. From time to time I would shoot into the palm of my hand and hungrily, greedily lap it all up, imagining it to be Joey's seed.

I watched for them day and night, listened for their car when they came home from work. I found any excuse to be outside when they were coming in or going out. I even started throwing the garbage out, religiously, much to my mom's surprise.

"Are you all right, Johnny?" She asked once, after a couple of weeks.

"Yeah! Why wouldn't I be?" I laughed at her as if she were being ridiculous.

"It's just that you're usually reluctant to do your chores," she replied. I rolled my eyes, sighed, and took the garbage out to the heavy-duty rubber cans at the side of the house.

Dad, however, was a bit more aware than he normally was. Something I had not given him enough credit for.

"I know what you're doing, son. You'd better be careful," he warned one Friday evening in mid-June.

"What are you talking about? I'm not doing anything!" I countered. But despite my attempts at denying my actions, my face gave me away. I felt myself blush at the realization that I might have been a little too obvious; even for my Dad!

I shook my head, ready to deny whatever it was he was going to confront me with. But nothing came out of my mouth. My throat was dry and scratchy.

Dad lowered his voice and whispered so that my mother wouldn't hear. "Don't tell your mother, but we've all had the same thoughts."

"We have?" *My dad? Thinking about Joey?* I stood there shocked.

Dad nodded his head. "Oh, yes. She's a dish, all right, and I can't even tell you how many of the men on this block alone would like a chance to boff her. *BUT* . . ." he warned. "She's married. Okay? I just want you to remember that. Your thoughts are yours to do with what you will, just don't do anything about them. Or do it with someone else. Understand?"

"Uh, yeah. Sure, Dad. Whatever you say," I replied with relief at his assumption that I had the hots for Angela. It was also the closest he ever came to talking to me about being a man and the responsibilities of sex.

That night, restless once again and unable to sleep, I had just jerked off a second time when I heard the car in their driveway, gravel crunching. I shot out of bed and pulled the chair out from my under my desk. Placing it in front of the window, I sat and waited. I don't know what for. I only knew that I wanted to see them at least getting out of their car.

The evening was unseasonably warm and as I sat there, a light sweat soon covered my body. I spread my legs wide and scratched at my balls, enjoying the way the sweat made them smell. I brought my fingers to my nose and inhaled deeply, then mouthed them and sucked on them.

The passenger door opened and Angela tumbled out, laughing giddily. Then the driver's door opened and Joey stepped out. I could only see their silhouettes. The alleyway between the two houses was all shadows. But I could see by the little bit of light that shone from the street lamp that he had taken his shirt off.

"So, do you wanna do it, or not?" I heard him ask softly, seductively.

"What, here?" She giggled. Joey shushed her.

"It was your idea. C'mere!" He whispered, his voice strong and determined.

"No!" She whispered coyly, heady from the booze she had obviously been drinking.

"Come over here!" Joey barked, and in an instant she stood before him. "Take your blouse off!" I watched in anticipation as her shadow slowly grabbed her top and pulled it up over head. She stood topless before him. Joey gave a little growl of pleasure and wrapped his arms around her. She moaned softly but I didn't know from what. Perhaps just from his touch.

Joey stepped back and I realized after a moment that he had undone his pants and pulled his cock out. I saw her silhouette sink to her knees and heard Joey moan. Then I heard the choking and gagging sounds of a mouth full of spit and wet cock. He started grunting steadily before he finally stopped and whispered sharply to her.

"Get up!"

"Why?" She whispered. "Don't you wanna shoot on my face the way you like to do?"

"No! I wanna fuck you now! Get up and sit on the car!"

Angela obeyed. She gave a slight jump and her silhouette landed softly on her behind, legs dangling over the side of the car, her breasts jiggling and swaying.

My dick was twitching anxiously by that point, wishing I was the one that was about to fuck her, that I could at least get a clear shot of his erect cock as it entered her. But the shadows were far too dark. All I could see was him moving closer to the edge of the car and her legs spreading as he entered her.

"Hmmmmm." Angela moaned loudly in the dark, leaning back until she was flat on the hood of the car. Joey held her legs spread wide, his large hands wrapped around her ankles.

"Ohhhhh, baby!" Joey whispered as he started fucking her. It seemed he was standing still, but I thought I saw much hip movement, thrusting back and forth, wiggling from side to side, filling her, screwing her, fucking her.

"Oh, Joey!" She moaned. "Your cock feels so good! Fuck me baby!" She whimpered and writhed on the car hood as Joey pumped her, fucking her on top of their car.

How I longed to be the one that was fucking her! I was so horny I grabbed a hold of my cock and squeezed it by the base. My balls ached but I didn't care. This was better than any fantasy I had ever had. I had no idea watching them could get me so hot.

Joey grunted and groaned, his hips moving faster. He started breathing heavy and I knew it wouldn't be long before he came inside her.

I stroked my cock faster, my balls bouncing heavily and smacking the chair. I wanted to time my climax with theirs, but then he stopped. I thought I heard a suction sound and then what sounded like a fart.

"Oh!" Angela cried. "I'm sorry! *That* was unexpected."

"That's what happens when you get fucked by such a huge cock," he muttered.

"I know, but it's so embarrassing."

"Don't worry, baby," he crooned. "It's not like I haven't heard your pussy farts before. Besides, I like feeling that gush of air against my meat as I pull it out. Now, get off the car and let's go upstairs. I wanna fuck you like a dog." He chuckled in the darkness and I watched his silhouette kiss her.

*Damn!* I muttered to myself. *Now I won't get to see anything! Shit! Fuck! Piss!*

I no longer felt like jerking off, although my dick throbbed and bounced up and down between my legs, demanding attention.

Their front door opened and closed and in the still silence of the night I heard their lock click. Disappointed, I stood up from my chair and slowly stretched as a soft breeze suddenly kicked in and wafted through my window. I stood there, feeling it lick and caress my body. It felt good on my aching balls and my still hard prick. Briefly I thought to grab a hold of it and shoot a load out the window, but decided against it. My fantasies couldn't compare to the actuality of watching them getting it on before my very eyes; even if the only thing I could see was their shadows and their bodies in silhouette.

I stepped away from the window and grabbed the back of the chair when a light went on in a room upstairs inside their house.

"Whoa! Now wait a minute!" I muttered aloud and sat back down on my chair.

Looking through their window, I found their bed suddenly illuminated. I had not realized before that I could see their bedroom from my window. My dick throbbed with the realization that I might be able to see them fucking right before my very eyes after all.

Angela laughed across the way as she came into full view of the window. She stood naked, every curve of her body clearly delineated in the light from the lamps on their night tables. She dropped the clothes in her hand to the floor and I watched as she lifted one hand up to her breasts while her other hand crept down her belly toward the hairy mound between her legs. I wanted to be there so badly I could almost taste it.

*How would it feel against my face?* I wondered. *How would it taste?* Guys on the swim team always boasted about eating pussy but how it was sometimes nasty if it smelled fishy. I took a deep breath of night air as if I could smell her from where I sat. Then I grabbed a hold of my cock and slowly started to stroke it.

Joey appeared, crawling on his knees, his head level with her pussy. I watched, enraptured, as he cupped her buttocks in his huge hands and thrust her hips forward until her pussy met his face. I thought I heard him inhale, then exhale with satisfaction. She moaned aloud as he opened his mouth and started to eat her. Her hands held the back of his head and she rotated her hips, grinding against him. He moaned as he tongued her, enjoying her gyrations as well as the feeling of her pubic hair against his face.

I was beside myself. I was so hot from what I was witnessing that I nearly came. I grit my teeth and scrunched my face against the overwhelming desire. My balls were really sore from the loads I'd shot before and the way they were bouncing up and down on the chair. I opened my eyes as the throbbing sensation began to subside. Releasing my cock, it bobbed up and down in the night air. I vowed not to touch it until they had come.

Angela moaned in disappointment as Joey pulled his face and mouth away from her pussy. He looked up at her and mouthed something that I couldn't hear. She nodded and stepped away from him. I watched her behind as she walked through a door and disappeared.

Joey stood. I gasped at the sight of his fully hard, rigid cock. In all my fantasies, I never envisioned him to be so thick and long; it looked bigger than mine.

Suddenly, I tried to move away from the window, but I was paralyzed. I could only sit there and watch as he stuck his head and torso out his bedroom window. He closed his eyes and took a deep breath of the night air, the breeze licking his body as it had done with mine. The sight of him, his arms, bulging and straining as he leaned forward, mesmerized me. He opened his eyes and seemed to look around. For a moment, I couldn't breath as he looked toward my bedroom window. I held my breath as if that would make me invisible.

*Could he see me?* I wondered. Then I thought, *Don't be ridiculous. The room is dark!* But if he couldn't see me, why did his sight linger at my window? Why did he pull back inside and reach for the blinds, then, as if thinking about it, left them alone?

Angela came back out, her body glistening, still wet from the shower she'd taken. She came to the window and wrapped her body around his. His arms imprisoned her in his hold, and I watched as his mouth sucked on her face, their tongues entwining. I could hear their moans and nearly died from desire. I felt my head grow faint and I wanted to cry out.

"Wait here," I heard him say, his voice husky as it had been the afternoon he knocked on my bedroom door.

"Hurry back," I heard her whisper.

"Yes! Hurry back," I whispered out loud.

Joey walked away and I watched the muscles of his round, firm, hairy ass. I longed to touch his buns, to bury my face between his crack and sniff the strong, sweaty, musky scent that I was sure his body gave off. I might have moaned from the thought because the next thing I knew, Angela had thrust her head and torso out through the window. She peered out in my direction. After a while, though, she closed her eyes and began to hum some secret melody, her hips moving softly, gently to and fro to her inner rhythm.

Her breasts hung down and I imagined myself on my back on the floor beneath her, breasts reaching down for my mouth. I would open my mouth and clamp my teeth around a nipple and chew on it, licking and squeezing both breasts as if trying to milk a cow.

A part of me couldn't help but wonder if it had all been planned. If they were putting on a show for my benefit.

I had thoughts of calling out to her, to let her know I could see them, ask if I could join them, but I knew I would never do it. It was just wishful thinking, merely a hungry cock longing for the touch of another human hand, craving the taste of flesh, tits, mouth, pussy, cock; anything that implied a body and sex and orgasm.

Angela was still leaning out the window, resting her face in her cupped hands when Joey came out of the bathroom. I watched in silence, enthralled with the sight of his pendulous cock swinging from side to side as he grew nearer, stiffening, bobbing, thickening.

She jumped, startled out of her reverie as Joey came up behind her. He stood to one side, his left hand caressing her buttocks, his right hand grabbing a hold of himself and pumping slowly. She attempted to get back inside, but he urgently held her in place.

"What the . . . ?" She asked, turning her head, but he reached out for her face and pushed it back so that she faced forward again. He reached up and started to close the window on top of her.

"Joey!" Angela protested, but the window had already come down on top of her. He moved behind her, grabbing her by the hips and pushed his cock inside. Her loud moan escaped her mouth, flew through the night air and across the alleyway at me. I could only begin to imagine what it felt like to be sliding into a moist, warm pussy already wet and excited from his tonguing. And then I briefly wondered what it would be like to have a pussy and be fucked from behind by something so large and thick.

Angela bit her lower lip, closed her eyes and tried to keep quiet, but the force of his thrusts as he buried himself deeper into her pussy, made her cry out. Soon she was moaning and squealing, unconcerned by the time of night, or the proximity of the houses.

"Oh . . . God ! . . . Joey!" Angela moaned, each sound separated by his thrusts. "I'm cuh . . . cuh . . . cuh . . ."

I watched in anticipation as he quickly pulled out of her and opened the window at the same time. He pulled her in, spun her around so that she was in profile, and sank to his knees before her. There, he buried his face in her crotch and greedily, almost in desperation, grunted wildly as he ground his face against her mound.

Angela screamed as she climaxed, juices flowing out of her, onto his tongue and into his mouth, filling his face with her scent. He didn't stop or release her until she seemed ready to collapse over his shoulder.

Grunting like an animal, Joey finally pulled away. I could see his profile, chin slick with pussy juice. I longed to lick it off him, wondering what it tasted like. Did it taste like pre-cum? Sperm? I sighed heavily and thought he might have heard; he shot a glance in my direction.

Joey stood up and kissed his wife. His hands went up to her shoulders and he started pushing her down. "Eat my meat, baby," he said, and guided her head.

"Yeah, yeah!" I whispered to myself in the darkness. My breath was starting to get harsh and raspy. Hungry for flesh, I opened my mouth and shoved my tongue out as far as it would go, as if I were the one about to lick his cock.

Angela sank to her knees and looked up at Joey. Her lips opened wide and wrapped around the bulging tip of his cock. He threw his head back and sucked his breath in as she cupped his balls. His hands wandered through her hair, squeezing her head as he thrust his hips into her mouth.

The very sight of that long shaft starting to slowly disappear into her mouth and down her throat nearly sent me into convulsions. But once again I held off. I didn't want to come yet. This was too good to be true and far too exciting to shoot off like that. I tried to look away, tried to think of something else so that I wouldn't get anymore excited than I already was, but I couldn't keep my eyes off that cock or off her lips. I longed to feel them on my own thick, throbbing erection, longed to feel that cock in my own mouth.

I watched as she moved back and forth, her lips sliding along the slick, wet shaft, yet never taking it all down her throat. I wondered if she would ever be able too. I had heard that some women didn't like to suck. Maybe it would hurt her tonsils. I stuck my fingers in my mouth and pushed them back as far as they would go until I gagged. I pulled my fingers out and looked at them. That wasn't very far down or very deep! I thought. There was no way she would be able to take him completely.

But I had underestimated the power, or perhaps willingness, of a horny man and a desirous woman. I watched as her throat seemed to swell as more and more of his cock disappeared in her mouth and down her throat. She bulged out like a frog croaking and his pubes smashed against her nostrils. She gagged loudly and spluttered, coughing as she pulled back. I could see her look up at him, her eyes filling with tears from the sensation of having her throat and mouth filled with so much meat.

Joey chuckled. "You should know better than that," he commented, and motioned for her to stand up. "Get on the bed." She started to lie down. "No! On your hands and knees!" He ordered her into the position he wanted.

Standing at the side of the bed, Joey stood behind Angela. I saw them in profile as he spread her cheeks and rubbed the head of his cock along the length of her crack. Angela moaned, then cried out as he entered her once again. He grunted and didn't stop until he had mounted her completely, sinking the entire length of his cock inside her warm, moist folds.

"Now, baby, I'm gonna fuck you," I could hear him mutter.

"Yes, Joey, yes! Fuck me!"

He pulled out, slowly at first, then slowly slid it back in. He increased his rhythm, working faster, harder, deeper. Angela grunted and groaned as her body was banged back and forth, her breasts swaying to and fro, her hair looking like the brushes in a car wash from the force of his thrusting hips. They rocked for a while, and then Joey, holding her in place, pulled out almost to the head. I watched as the entire thing slid back inside her, disappearing as quickly as it had come out. He pushed it all the way in and continued pushing while pulling her back towards him as if he wanted his whole body to disappear inside her.

Angela fingered herself and screamed as she climaxed a second time.

Joey pulled his hard cock out of her, slick and slimy.

"Lick it off!" He cried. Angela quickly spun around and licked his cock like a lollipop. When she'd sucked her juices off his cock, he stepped back and walked to the foot of the bed. There, he turned around so that he faced the window and sat down. He lay on his back and held his cock up by the base, waving it at her and at me, as well, I suppose. At that point, I was so into their fucking I could have cared less if they knew I was watching.

"Climb on top of me, babe! Ride me!" Angela willingly obliged. She turned around, her ass toward me, and straddled him. She grabbed his cock halfway down the shaft, while he held it up for her by the base. Then she started the long descent down until she was sitting completely on his groin. His balls bulged from her weight, his cock deeply set and buried up inside her snatch. She started rocking while his hips wiggled, grinding up and down. She moaned with the feeling of him up inside her and I could almost hear him breathing heavily. Then he started grunting.

I grabbed a hold of my still rock hard cock and started stroking it again. Just the very touch of my fingers on the warm, throbbing shaft nearly set me off. Yet, somehow, once again I held back. I didn't want to shoot yet. I wanted to come with him.

I sat there in the dark, stroking myself, watching anxiously as she rocked back and forth, from side to side, then slid up and down on Joey's shaft so that I could see every glorious inch appear and reappear.

"Get off!" He cried. "Get on your back and spread your legs!"

Angela, in the throes of desire, leapt off her husband and rolled onto her back. She all but disappeared from view. All I could see was her right leg as she spread them.

"No! NO!" I whispered aloud.

"C'mere! Slide down!" Joey stood up and shot a glance towards the window.

Angela scooted over and came back into view. Joey turned her around and pushed her onto her back so that she was flat, her head hanging over the foot of the bed. He spread her legs and hooked them over his shoulders. I watched his cock disappear inside her again. He thrust it in and out roughly, harshly, slamming her as if he were punishing her. All the while, he was looking out his window, towards mine, and I knew then he was doing it all for my benefit.

*But why?* I wondered. Then decided I didn't care. I was just grateful to see it all.

I pumped my cock as feverishly as he pumped his into her.

"Oh! . . . Joey!" Angela started, just as she had done before she had her first orgasm.

"Let it go, baby! I'm not far behind!"

"Me either!" I whispered out into the dark.

Joey pumped and pumped, thrusting in and out, his hips gyrating back and forth and then in a corkscrew motion every time he sank back in up to the balls. Then, with a final thrust, Joey grunted and growled. It was a loud and uninhibited sound, like a wounded animal crying out to the world to witness his pain; except that he couldn't be in pain. Of that I was sure.

He pulled his cock out of her pussy. It pulsated, squirting a heavy, steamy load all over her bush. I was enraptured by the sight of his angry, red cock, come squirting like pumping blood out of it. My vision seemed to zoom in on the sight of it and I groaned as I, too, came and shot a bigger load than I had previously that night. My balls ached even more than before as they churned more and more sperm out of the sac. I sat in my chair, my pumping fist still stroking, my body convulsing from the force of my climax. My heart beat loudly in my head, and slowly, gently, it began to subside.

I opened my eyes to see Joey on his knees, his mouth on her bush, eating his come.

"Oh, man!" I moaned and once again wished I could be there to taste her pussy juice, lick it off his cock and taste his come on her mound, licking and feeling the wiry pubic hair flossing between my teeth. I consoled myself by licking the come off my hand and catching the dripping juice from my shaft onto my fingers. I sucked at them greedily, hungry with the hope that someday soon I would be able to experience flesh rather than just fantasize about it.

As I stood up from my chair to put it back, I heard Angela's voice. "I'm going to go clean up."

Joey grunted in response, leaning his body against the window frame. His cock glistened, loosing its tumescence in an achingly slow way.

"Pssst!" I heard after she had disappeared from view. I stood still, unsure of what to do. "Pssstt!" The sound came again, this time louder, more insistent. "Johnny!" I pretended I couldn't hear him. "I know you're there. I can see your shadow! It's okay, man! We get off on being watched."

I stuck my head out the window. A slow, sexy grin spread across his face. There was a hard glint in his eye. "So?" Joey chuckled. "Did you enjoy it?"

It took me a long moment before I responded. I stuck my head out the window. "I sure did!" I croaked, my voice nervous and excited.

"She's even better in person. How'd you like to have a go at her? I bet you'd like that, wouldn't you, mister jock swimmer?" He teased.

"Would I!" I mustered.

"She's got this thing for big meat. Think you can handle it? You got a big one?"

"Not as big as yours," I replied nervously.

"I'm sure it's big enough. She likes being plugged at both ends with big cocks." Joey grinned. "Go to bed. We'll talk some more soon. Good night, buddy."

"Good night," I replied, and watched him disappear. The lights in their bedroom went off and I was left in total silence and darkness.

I got up and crawled into bed with exhaustion. My balls throbbed and ached with a dull sensation, but I didn't care. I felt satisfied for the first time in a long while.

*What else could I guy ask for?* I thought to myself, and drifted to sleep.

Visit the author at:
www.horndawgz.blogspot.com

www.ingramcontent.com/pod-product-compliance
Lightning Source LLC
Chambersburg PA
CBHW020622250626
47154CB00004B/1620